A MOST DETERMINED LUNATIC

a novel based on true events

by

Steven R. Garman

Cover design and graphic layout by Steven Garman
Author photograph by Barbara Wright
Cover photos licensed from Getty Images

© 2015 Steven R. Garman / Scarlett Media
All Rights Reserved
Printed in the United States of America

Library of Congress Cataloging-in-Publication Data
Garman, Steven R.
The book "A Most Determined Lunatic – A Novel Based on True Events"

Paperback ISBN: 978-0-578-18050-2
1st Edition – January 2016 – Drama
Time specific nonexclusive world paperback distribution rights:
        Amazon.com

A special thank you for his invaluable assistance in editing this book goes to Brian Sink, who faithfully reviewed the manuscript, offered encouragement and helped mold it into the work that it is today. I owe him a great debt for his dedication, insight and support.

For Jane, Whitney and Lane:
my truly wonderful family

ONE

It is February 1990 and an unusually warm day in the Dallas-Fort Worth area. The guest in room 115 has been camped out at the La Quinta Inn on State Road 183 in Hurst, Texas, for more than two weeks. He rarely leaves the motel and doesn't want a maid. When he does leave his room it's to restock at the liquor store, get a sandwich out of the cooler at the 7-Eleven across the street, or pick up a prostitute for an hour of entertainment.

Every couple days, he also leaves the hotel to score drugs to feed his ravenous appetite for cocaine. He has already lost his wife, his daughter, his estate home and a high-profile job that pays well because he just can't quit.

Tonight he's on the prowl for both a good time and a big high. The La Quinta maintenance man has tipped him to a drug dealer in Watauga, a sad incorporated area of small older homes, rundown warehouses and low-income apartments just north of Fort Worth, about fifteen minutes away. The dealer reportedly has a large supply of high-quality powder, at a price only slightly higher than outrageous.

The first shadows of the fast-approaching night are just starting to fall as the addict pulls his car down Fleming Drive and parks in front of a small, marginally maintained ranch home. A brand-new, extensively customized Ford 150 truck is conspicuously parked in the driveway, and a large man in his late 30s wearing a Dallas Cowboys jersey gets out. A deal is quickly struck for $500 of fine white flakes.

Having scored enough "bazooka" — an extremely powerful form of powdered cocaine — to last several days, the addict turns his attention to finding a playmate for the rest of the evening. He knows exactly where to go because he has cruised the sprawling parking lot of the Stop-n-Go Truck Stop on Route 820 just south of the old North Hills Mall in Richland Hills several times in the past two weeks. But this night is different. He has a gnawing sexual hunger, and there is a near panic urgency to his search.

A MOST DETERMINED LUNATIC

* * *

The addict and his new best friend, a slightly overweight 40ish black woman named DaVita, who goes by the street name Sparkle, have been partying in room 115 for half an hour when things turn ugly. Too much booze and cocaine has soured the already sullen addict's mood by several shades of mean.

Sparkle is reclining nude on the rumpled bed, trying to recover from an extremely rough romp in the sheets, while her client downs the last of a mixture of cocaine and vodka from a plastic water bottle. Sparkle is a seasoned pro, but her client seems to have an unusually ravenous sexual appetite, especially for an overweight guy in his 40s. Sitting silently across the room, he stares at her for several minutes. After popping another small tablet of speed, the addict is suddenly back on top of her, roughly fondling her breast.

"Hey man, give me a minute here, will ya?" Sparkle pleads. "You done whacked me out, baby." She tries in vain to push the overweight man off her stomach, but the addict blurts out, "Bitch, I own you," and gives her a sucker punch to her temple.

For the next several minutes, he pummels the semi-conscious prostitute until her face is an unrecognizable, bloodied mess. He pins her to the bed and ravages her until he is satisfied yet again. Beaten and brutalized, Sparkle has no defense for the animal-like attack. Then an eight-inch, ultra-sharp swing-blade knife appears, slowly slicing a thin cut down her abdomen toward her crotch. Sparkle's garbled screams go unheard as the knife repeatedly circles her firm silicone breasts and finds a soft spot between her ribs.

* * *

The lunatic from room 115 is more than just a demented drunk and ticking time bomb. He is also a small-time arms dealer. He has built a profitable cash-only side business supplying modified weapons to a discriminating criminal clientele of drug dealers, pimps and survival fanatics.

From his temporary corporate headquarters in the La Quinta Inn, he makes regular sales demonstrations to a steady stream of malcontents looking to purchase customized firearms or black-market ammunition. On this occasion, he is meeting a potential customer known as King Wiz who has an interest in obtaining a fully automatic AK-47 for personal protection. King Wiz has a lucrative drug business, and occasionally he needs to enforce the terms of a purchase agreement with a high-powered firearm. After a brief discussion and examination of a dozen items, the drug dealer selects an Albanian-made Type 56 AK-47 that was originally built on a Chinese tooling template. The weapon has been extensively modified, featuring a pistol grip rather than the conventional folding metal stock, a shortened barrel and the capability of firing on full automatic. The gun provides more lethal power than King Wiz will ever need and requires more skill to operate than he will ever possess.

After a brief discussion about the pistol's nomenclature, King Wiz demands a live ammo demonstration. This goes against the terms of the seller's standard purchasing contract. He doesn't like to have guns and ammo in close proximity to each other when dealing with a new client. Too many bad things can happen. His MO is to show a weapon to a potential buyer, and they take his word regarding performance. He might be a drunk and a doper, but when it comes to arms sales, his word is good, and he has a list of satisfied customers to attest to his reliability and workmanship.

King Wiz insists on a demo, and the seller needs some quick cash, so he allows King Wiz to provide a non-refundable $500 cash deposit, with $1,000 more if the gun performs as advertised. The weapons dealer will bring the merchandise, along with fifty rounds of ammunition, to a secluded wooded area near the Cider Creek Reservoir off State Road 175 about an hour south of Dallas. They will meet at dusk and test-fire the AK-47.

Although often dulled by alcohol or drugs, the weapons dealer's mental acuity is generally on full alert when selling dangerous firearms to unsavory characters. This deal is no exception. He arrives an hour early at the meeting location to case the surroundings, checking possible escape paths and parking his car so it's headed toward the best route to the interstate. Last, he plants a fully loaded submachine gun behind a large boulder near his car.

He doesn't like what he sees when his client pulls up to the rendezvous site in a shiny new Cadillac. King Wiz isn't alone, as had been agreed. A muscle-bound black man who seems to emit ill intent from every pore in his rock-hard body is behind the wheel. The weapons dealer goes on high alert as his eyes jump back and forth between the drug king and his hired help.

Upon exiting the car, the drug czar signals his sinister-looking friend to search the weapons dealer. Satisfied that he's not carrying a concealed weapon, the rent-a-thug steps back, and King Wiz demands the AK-47 to examine it. "Let's see the goodies, Cracker. You know this thing better do the dirty deed, brother, or you've wasted my time, and I ain't into people wasting my time."

The ominous-looking weapon is laid out on a blue blanket on the ground, along with a banana clip of high-velocity ammo. As King Wiz and his companion move in to examine their purchase, the arms dealer slowly begins stepping backward toward his car. He has been intently watching the body language of the thugs and has a bad feeling about this group. He has no interest in being caught off guard.

King Wiz picks up the weapon and slams in the clip, letting out a long, high-pitched whistle. "Oh momma! This is one sweet-assed tool."

With that he fires off a burst of rounds that shred a nearby sapling while screaming over the gunfire, "Shit yes! Holy shit! Yes! Yes! Yes!" As the clip empties, a thick, blue smoke fills the clearing and partially obscures the drug dealer, but he can still be seen and is nodding to his associate, who begins reaching under his jacket.

Forewarned by the henchman's movement, the salesman dives behind the boulder and comes up with the planted machine gun. He doesn't wait to see what the muscleman planned to do before squeezing off a volley that saws him nearly in half. King Wiz stands frozen with the assault weapon in his hands before he too is felled by the explosive impact of a dozen hollow-point rounds.

Before the gun smoke clears, the arms dealer strips the bodies of their gold chains, identification and cash, recovers the AK-47 and removes the Caddy's license plate. As he guns his car toward the highway, in the rearview mirror he can see an orange ball of flame that was once a Cadillac shoot into the dark sky. The cops will write off the carnage as a drug deal gone bad and privately be pleased that King Wiz is no longer a problem.

* * *

The metallic, copper-brown 1989 Mercury Grand Marquis slowly rolls down the steep grade of the street barely six inches from the curb. The engine is off, and despite the heat of the day, all the deeply tinted windows are up. The dirty two-door silently coasts to a stop where Mockingbird Lane and Saddlebrook Drive form a T. Once parked, the driver slumps down in the front seat as if to settle in for a long wait. He is alone, and the car is filled with trash.

Mockingbird Lane is lined with majestic oak trees and upper-middle-class, two-story brick homes, most with electric driveway gates and rock-lined swimming pools. The school bus from the Colleyville Independent School District has already zigzagged through the lazy Texas neighborhood depositing its cargo of future business executives and beauty pageant contestants. Homework complete, boys race bicycles in the streets and girls practice cheerleading in the front yards.

The driver of the Mercury doesn't seem to notice the youthful exuberance as he stares with bloodshot eyes across the intersection at 704 Saddlebrook Drive. He only occasionally blinks as he peers out over gold-rimmed aviator sunglasses pushed well down on his nose. The focal point of his surveillance is a brick Georgian plantation-style home with four two-story white pillars across the large front porch. A new deep-maroon Plymouth Grand Voyager — the Colleyville soccer mom's ride of choice — is parked in the drive. The manicured front yard is as green as a golf-course, with neatly trimmed shrubs and colorful flowerbeds lining the circular drive.

Without looking away from the home's leaded-glass front doors, the driver reaches across the front seat littered with fast-food sacks and candy bar wrappers to grab a plastic bottle containing a toxic mixture of vodka and cocaine. After taking a deep gulp from the bottle, he allows it to rest on his lower lip for several moments while he continues staring at the house. The driver is so consumed by his surveillance that he is oblivious that the car windows are rolled up and the air conditioning is off on an 86-degree day. The driver doesn't seem to notice as beads of sweat cascade down his forehead and pool under his chin, soaking the collar of his flowered Hawaiian shirt. Despite the heat, he is wearing a tweed sport coat. His dilated pupils are as big as saucers, and he rarely moves. He is on a mission.

A MOST DETERMINED LUNATIC

* * *

At about 5:15 p.m., Katherine Osborne, a widowed 53-year-old retired elementary school teacher, looks out a front window of her home on Mockingbird Lane and sees the brown Mercury that she has seen stalking the neighborhood twice before. She watches the car for several minutes before picking up the phone and calling the Colleyville Police Department to report the suspicious car parked in front of her house. Corporal Darrel Ward, a four-year veteran of the force, is cruising just blocks away when he receives the call from the dispatcher; within minutes, he is pulling down Mockingbird Lane. Ward flips on the red-and-blue light bar on the roof of the patrol car and parks just a few feet off the back bumper of the Mercury. He briefly observes the man in the front seat, and his trained instincts kick into overdrive. Grabbing his service cap off the front seat and unsnapping the restraining strap on his .38-caliber police special revolver, he gets out of the patrol car and raps forcefully on the driver's window. Receiving no acknowledgment, the patrolman pounds again on the window, hard enough that the glass vibrates. There is still no movement inside the car. Sensing the situation has started badly and probably won't get better soon, Ward snatches the mic from his patrol belt and sternly tells the dispatcher to send backup, quickly.

Suddenly, the Mercury starts with a jolt but then moves forward very slowly, creeping toward the intersection. Ward yells at the driver to stop, but the car continues to roll slowly around the corner and onto Saddlebrook Drive. The car is moving so slowly that Corporal Ward simply walks along beside the driver's door, screaming and pounding on the glass.

At this point, patrol Sergeant Randy Ortiz arrives in his black-and-white Ford Explorer, just in time to observe the bizarre chase moving down Saddlebrook Drive at three miles an hour. Ortiz pulls his vehicle around the lumbering Mercury and forces it toward the curb less than two blocks from where the chase began. As Ortiz jumps out of his patrol car with gun drawn, Ward grabs the driver's side door handle and jerks it open.

The driver barely reacts as Ward reaches in and begins pulling him through the car door toward the street. Then, without warning, the driver becomes a wild man with incredible strength, wedging himself against the Mercury's doorframe. Ward frantically calls out to Ortiz, "Help me, Randy. This guy is going Superman on me." Ortiz holsters his weapon as he advances to the car and grabs the wild man's arm, twisting it as hard as he can for leverage. "This guy must be on PCP," Ortiz yells back to Ward as the driver flicks him off as if he were a fly.

The two cops struggle with the wild man for several minutes before they force him out of the car and get him face down on the street. "Grab his feet! Grab his feet, Randy!" Ward pleads as he sprawls out flat on the driver's back, pinning his arms to his side. Ortiz falls on the driver's thrashing feet to keep him from kicking his heels back on Ward. Several more minutes pass before the two winded officers finally get handcuffs on their prisoner and feel he is secure enough that they can stop to catch their breath.

"Holy crap, Ward," Ortiz wheezes as he stands in the middle of the street, bent over at the waist with his hands on his hips. "Why in the hell didn't you tell me this guy is the Incredible Hulk in disguise?" Ward, still sitting on the ground next to the freshly subdued wild man jabs back, "Well, Sergeant Ortiz, if you would have gotten here in time to be of any real help, I would have." Ortiz straightens up and with a slight smirk says, "Well, then Corporal, you can put Mr. Hulk in the back of my car by yourself." Ward looks down at his still-struggling prisoner and says, "I doubt it. And I think the Hulk's name might be Holloway. It's on this letter I just found in the pocket of his sport coat."

TWO

Joseph Vincent Holloway was born in Tulsa, Oklahoma, on July 22, 1944, the second of two sons born to, but not particularly wanted by, Rolland and Vonda Holloway. He grew up in a weathered one-story, four-room rental on the wrong side of the tracks in a family continually engulfed in tension. Rolland drank — a lot — and his primary occupation was welfare. A New Yorker by birth, he was out of place and unhappy in Tulsa, and alcohol helped him forget his troubles, of which there were many. Vonda Stone was a shy girl of limited motivation who met Rolland at a movie theater and later agreed to marry him because she had nothing better to do.

In short order Vonda gave birth to two boys, and the kids drove Rolland nuts. He would come home in the evening after a hard day of working on a bottle of whiskey at the local strip club and rain abuse on his family. Vonda never stood up to him, and she never took the boys' side when Rolland bullied and belittled them. Whenever she spoke out against Rolland or mentioned any of his numerous failures, he punched her, usually more than once, so she elected to become invisible.

And then she left altogether. After four years of marriage Vonda had two sons, no job, few prospects and a divorce decree. Leaving Tulsa in a battered old Chevy pickup pulling a small rental trailer, Vonda set out with her few possessions and two shell-shocked young boys for a better life in New Orleans, where her brother lived and ran a small business. After camping for a couple nights at a girlfriend's house, she used welfare money to rent a two-room flat on North Rocheblave Street in the Lower Ninth Ward, a few blocks from the Inner Harbor navigation canal. Little Joe spent a lot of his free time recklessly riding a stolen bike along the ledge of the canal, stopping every now and then to throw rocks at the homeless drunks who lived there. He hated his life, but at least his father didn't beat him anymore.

Joe grew up idolizing his older brother, Ronald, who was everything he was not: athletic, outgoing, smart and good-looking. Ron excelled in school and had lots of friends. He would graduate with honors from Tulane University Law School, marry a well-scrubbed Metairie Country Club debutante and go on to be a respected real estate attorney in Florida.

But Joe accomplished nothing like that. He languished in school and had few friends and no direction. Lacking the grades for college, he enlisted in the Army and was sent to Fort Sam Houston in San Antonio for training as a combat medical specialist.

Joe had never been to Texas, but he had always been intrigued by its history, especially the armed conflict with Mexico. Soon after arriving at Fort Sam Houston he visited the Alamo, and he found the military connection with the evolution of San Antonio fascinating. "Fort Sam" was named for the U.S. senator, Texas governor and first president of the Republic of Texas, and had been deeded by San Antonio to the Army with 93 acres of land in the 1870s.

In San Antonio, combat medic Joe Holloway was taught to draw blood, start an IV, treat gunshot wounds and splint broken bones. He mastered the finer points of stretcher etiquette. And he learned how to steal pharmaceuticals. The neophyte medics learned how to give shots by practicing on each other using saline in the syringes, unless they were druggies. In their case, they used narcotics stolen from the base pharmacy and shot their own arms full of dope. Joe did not mind the duty, and he enjoyed the drugs and was pleased to have more freedom than the average infantry grunt. Lucking out after his training was completed, he was sent to Germany rather than combat in Vietnam and realized that being a medic had some real advantages.

Joe was assigned to the thousand-bed U.S. Army 97th General Hospital in Frankfurt and spent the next year and a half treating the sprained ankles, blood blisters and broken bones of training troops. The duty was easy, the beer was good, and the frauleins were friendly.

As a medic, Joe was almost adequate. He was promoted to private first class but lost that rank when on a drunken bender he took a jeep and drove it without shifting until the transmission blew out. He cultivated a passion for dangerous weapons, something the military didn't necessarily discourage, cherishing the opportunity to play with guns or knives, the bigger the better. He started buying revolvers and soon had a small arsenal of weapons in his footlocker. He also began hanging out with a group of fellow underachieving soldiers who passionately embraced a militaristic survivalist mentality. Most of Joe's free time was spent drinking, going to gun shows and visiting the drug-addicted women at the rundown brothel near the base. After three years, the Army decided they could manage without Joe, and he was honorably discharged back to a dead-end civilian life.

In May 1966, Joe was hired as a milkman by the Borden Company and entrusted with a truck route. Joe's contribution to the company was lackluster, and he was fired in less than a year. Soon after that, he became a lineman on a repair crew with the South Central Bell Telephone Company. Risking his life restoring downed power lines paid better than delivering milk, but it was equally boring to Joe, so in July 1967 he quit the phone company and enrolled in the University of New Orleans as a part-time student with an undeclared major. But school was still not his strong suit, and he dropped out after a couple of mediocre semesters and went back to work.

In 1969, Joe found something he was reasonably good at when he accepted a job as a ballpoint pen salesman with the Paper Mate Division of the Gillette Company. He did well enough not to get fired but left after two years feeling unappreciated and underpaid. A few months later, he thought he'd hit a home run when he landed a position with Lozier Store Fixtures selling shelving and display cases. The job paid well, and the owner's daughter, who worked as the company's receptionist, was a real looker. Jenny Lozier, however, thought Joe Holloway was a low-life and rejected his advances. As a result, he allowed his temper to get the better of him, verbally sparring with

Jenny's father, once almost punching him. Joe once again departed an excellent opportunity before establishing himself, feeling superior to those he left behind.

In the past, Joe had been able to land a series of good jobs despite being average. He was short and overweight and a bit slow on the uptake, but he represented himself well during interviews and was always impeccably dressed. His slow drawl gave the appearance of being deliberate and thoughtful when really he was just slow to respond. After walking away from the job at Lozier Store Fixtures, he half-heartedly looked for a new job for about a month, then settled into a daily routine of drinking himself numb.

After six months in a drunken stupor, Joe finally sobered up enough to land a sales job with Fleet Guard Inc., a preventive maintenance company selling products and services to large industrial fleet operators. Joe surprised himself and did well at the job, but he never made the connection that it was because he had cut down on drinking and self-medication. He honed his sales skills on the road and eventually got a promotion to sales manager of the fleet's five-man sales force. Joe was now a bona fide business executive and proud of it. His good fortune continued when he met a mousey young lady who found him handsome and worldly.

Melissa Gier was as painfully shy as she was sweet. Barely five feet tall and plain as a manila envelope, she had slipped through high school almost totally unnoticed. She was smart and quick with numbers, so after graduation she was content to work a dead-end bookkeeping job and keep her head down, preferring to tackle a balance sheet than talk to co-workers.

Melissa met Joe by accident in the campus cafeteria at Loyola University, where Joe had enrolled in a business development night class. Although not a student, Melissa would occasionally eat an evening sack in the dining hall and spend the rest of the night in the library. She had never been into the dating scene but was lonely and secretly hoped to find a Big Easy Prince Charming. So it was no surprise that, upon bumping into a well-dressed businessman at the snack bar, she was immediately swept off her feet. It was a major breakthrough for her when the dapper and self-proclaimed master business executive noticed her. She welcomed the attention.

Joe mesmerized Melissa with fiction about his heroic exploits in the Army and wild success as a dynamic businessman. Soon they were dating, and Joe stayed on his best behavior, most of the time. Within a year they were married in a private ceremony at City Hall in New Orleans. Melissa wore a simple pale-yellow dress that she borrowed from her sister and carried a small bouquet of white magnolias bought by her brother-in-law. Joe showed up ten minutes late and a little drunk in a dark-blue rented tux. Shortly after returning from a weekend honeymoon in Lake Charles, the newlyweds set up housekeeping in a nondescript little bungalow in Harahan, Louisiana. Joe got another promotion to general manager at Fleet Guard. With Melissa's steady paycheck rolling in and savings from his management job, Joe gave college another try. Because he still needed two years to complete a degree, he abruptly quit work and enrolled full-time at Loyola University as a psychology major. Melissa was markedly disappointed in his decision; he had not even bothered to discuss it with her.

This time around, Joe was more focused and by January 1976, he had earned a bachelor of science degree in psychology with a minor in business management. But when he did not immediately find a suitable job for someone of what he believed was his superior intellect and lofty stature, he began hanging out at a local watering hole between interviews, where he ran into an old Army buddy. Lucas Westwright had been dishonorably dismissed from the Army for robbing the base post exchange shortly after Joe was discharged. As a master thief, Lucas was a complete failure. While in the service, he had been caught three times stealing supplies. After a couple of demotions and one summary court martial, the Army invited him to leave. Soon he and Joe were regularly meeting at The Shot Glass in Slidell, hatching masterful business plans that had no chance of seeing the light of day.

Drinking led to swapping war stories, which led to drinking more, which led to swapping survival tips. Lucas told Joe about a group of friends he partied with on weekends who really knew how to have a good time. Soon, Joe was running around in the delta in surplus Army fatigues, face greased green and black, with a few dozen other gun-toting zealots. Deadly weapons were everywhere, and not just your average run-of-the-mill AK-47 assault rifles. These guys had big-boy toys: Chinese MP18 submachine guns, French MAC19 light-tank guns, a Nazi Gewehr 98 sniper rifle, a couple cases of British No. 76 Hawkins anti-tank grenades, and of course the must-have at any survivalist get-together, an Uncle Sam's M1A1 flame-thrower. To many die-hard survivalists, there is something special about sitting around a roaring campfire in the middle of the bayou late at night drinking until you're totally wasted. The drinking would bring out the paranoia in Joe, but it was tolerated because he was in his element hanging out with nonconformist malcontents and underachievers. They respected his don't-give-a-shit attitude and valued his ability to score quality dope and high-powered weapons. He had found soul mates.

A MOST DETERMINED LUNATIC

THREE

At 6 feet 2½ inches and 210 pounds, Sawyer Rolston Graham was a fit 36-year-old former big man on campus and present-day business executive. Sonny, as he was known by almost everyone, was director of sales for Omniplex Worldwide's U.S. Medical Instrument Division. Omniplex was a Japanese-owned international conglomerate, and everyone in the company's Dallas office knew Sonny was a superstar destined for bigger things.

Born and raised in northern Indiana, he had a quiet Hoosier calm and self-confident demeanor that went well with his boyish good looks, sharp intellect, quick wit and dry sense of humor.

Sonny grew up in a small three-bedroom ranch-style home on the edge of Goshen, a sleepy small-college town surrounded by cornfields and Amish buggies. His parents —Wayne and Eileen — were hard-working, friendly people who tried diligently to raise their two children to be respectable contributors to society. Sonny's younger sister Lynn was the true intellect of the family. A diminutive dynamo, she was cute and knew it, and Sonny played the protective big brother when necessary. And though most of the time he pretended to be indifferent to her, Sonny in fact secretly admired Lynn's brains and spunk.

Sonny was a bright kid but not stuffy or bookish. He was extremely well-organized when he set his mind to accomplishing a task and could focus on a goal like a laser. Quiet at first when working with strangers, he was a natural leader who would usually be drafted by his peers for a leadership role. Sonny's easy manner and solid work ethic, combined with a teaching spirit, made him a willing mentor to those around him.

Throughout high school, Sonny didn't care much for scholastics and never broke a sweat studying. As a perennial teacher's pet he made average grades with little effort and was content to excel at extracurricular activities. His duties as senior class president, president of the student counsel and booster club, and president of the county Junior Achievement program were laced around marching in the school band, presiding as master councilor of the local DeMolay chapter, playing a lot of pick-up sports and serving as an usher at the Lutheran church.

Sonny had an entrepreneurial spirit and was ambitiously self-motivated. In his spare time, he ran a profitable cash-only business making handmade signs promoting the city's youth recreation center and after-game dances at the high school. He was occasionally hired to paint signs for retail stores and auto dealerships and drew a cartoon that ran in a local advertising monthly. By sixteen he was a successful businessman just like his dad.

Wayne Graham was a self-made man, having grown up in a small Indiana farm town that had two options for graduating high school boys: plant corn, or join the military. World War II was raging when he graduated, so Wayne married Eileen, his high school sweetheart, and immediately enlisted in the Army as a baker.

He was sent to Fort MacArthur in California, where he was stationed for the rest of the war, as a perforated eardrum gifted to him by his younger brother, Red, during a youthful fistfight, kept him stateside. After the war ended, Wayne and Eileen moved back to Indiana, where he bounced through a couple of low-paying jobs before becoming a fork-lift driver on the loading dock of a large industrial rubber company. Thirty years and two children later, Wayne was vice president of sales and production at a thriving multi-million-dollar manufacturing company headquartered in Goshen.

Sonny inherited his father's business drive and savvy, but before becoming a corporate bigwig he had to get through college. A year at the local Mennonite college proved unrewarding. Sonny found the administration's draconian policies and religious fervor insufferable, and he felt he had nothing in common with the other 913 captive undergrads. On top of that, he was uncomfortably living at home with his parents while all his buddies went off to Ball State or Purdue or Indiana to frolic with sorority girls and drink beer until they passed out. He didn't try to fit in at Goshen College, but he couldn't leave in his first year because he had received several small civic club scholarships that were good only there. An unfortunate financial setback had left his family temporarily without the money to send Sonny away to a state college. Still, Sonny was grateful to be able to go to college, even if it meant working nights and attending Mennonite chapel every morning before class.

By the end of Sonny's freshman year, his father's finances had stabilized enough, and he was paroled to Indiana University in Bloomington, in the southern part of the state. Sonny left for IU under the release conditions set by his parents that he must work part-time to help with expenses. He arrived on campus in a used but well-preserved 1962 midnight-blue two-door Chevy Malibu — christened by a friend as "the Babemobile" — that he bought with his savings and graduation gift cash. He pledged Theta Chi fraternity, was elected president of the 24-member pledge class, and declared as a business administration and management major in the business school without giving much thought about studying anything else. Life was good, and the grades were fair.

Sonny had no trouble meeting the terms of his parole, working in IU's Athletic Department selling sports tickets to students and the public. He logged more time at the ticket office than he did in the classroom and soon was running part of the operation by himself, falling into a comfortable routine: Work a lot, drink frequently, date occasionally and attend class rarely. The ticket office gave Sonny not just spending money, but also an excellent opportunity to meet an endless supply of perky co-eds buying student passes to university events. He dated a series of interchangeable college girls, most of whom were more interested in partying than hitting the books.

One of Sonny's rambunctious dates earned him a place in Theta Chi folklore. He and a particular top-heavy blonde had gone up to his room in the fraternity house to study a bottle of vodka. After a couple drinks, Sonny's date attempted to sit on the sill of an open window but tumbled backward onto the front porch roof. She was too drunk to get hurt by the three-foot fall, but she made history when she popped up in all her topless glory in front of the high-intensity flood lights aimed at the front porch. With her considerable assets on full display she waved to startled passersby below. "I'm okay," she reassured, "but I peed my pants." The humor of the event escaped a campus safety officer who was driving by as Ms. Congeniality sprang up on the roof, and Sonny's evening ended with a private meeting at campus police headquarters, certainly not what he had envisioned when the "study date" had begun. In the end, Sonny got a warning, and Blondie got her blouse back.

As time passed, Sonny began to see college as more than just a long party punctuated by work and an occasional semester exam. He studied more and attended classes semi-regularly instead of rarely. As his grades improved, he once again immersed himself in extracurricular activities. Sonny was elected president of the fraternity, a delegate to the IU Student Government Board and a representative to the Interfraternity Council. He joined the Young Republicans Club on campus and became campus coordinator for William D. Ruckelshaus's losing Congressional bid, using his position to make valuable connections that would serve him well years later when Richard Nixon named Ruckelshaus assistant attorney general of the United States.

As Sonny drifted toward graduation in his senior year, he began to think about life after college. He would have a bachelor of science degree in business management with minors in marketing and advertising but no real clue what he really wanted to do. A fraternity brother and good friend, Wes Hampton, had gone into sales with Owens Corning Fiberglas, a large building materials company headquartered in Toledo, Ohio, and suggested Sonny interview with the company. Wes would grease the interviewing skids, so Sonny took him up on the offer. The grease worked: A brief campus interview led to a group interview, which led to a third meeting with a couple of suits from the company's regional office at an expensive restaurant in downtown Indianapolis. And in late May at a private dinner in Toledo with the national sales manager, Sonny accepted a field sales position with Owens Corning's new Supply and Contracting Division. He had envisioned being stationed in an exotic location like Hawaii but was offered Indianapolis instead. Naptown, as it was known for its sleepy reputation, was definitely not Hawaii, but at least it wasn't Fargo or Billings, either, and the city hosted the world's biggest auto race, the Indianapolis 500, on Memorial Day weekend every year. The whole month of May in Indianapolis was one big party. Because of his long-standing interest in anything having to do with the Indy 500, Sonny took the job thinking it wouldn't be bad at all; at least he could stop at the speedway after work when there was activity on the track.

Sonny had stumbled into a premier, good-paying sales position with a major company without any heavy lifting. He would miss his fraternity comrades and the weekend parties with frisky sorority sisters, but he knew he couldn't stay in college forever. So it was, "Good-bye Indiana University, hello business world."

FOUR

In the summer of 1969, Sonny received two noteworthy letters on the same day. One was a welcome from the president of Owens Corning Fiberglas, retired Gen. Lauris Norstad, who was also a former head of NATO. The other was a draft notice.

It was hard to get excited about the first while reading the second.

The Vietnam War was seething in Southeast Asia, and it had a major impact on the mood of the country, especially young Americans like Sonny. Uncle Sam was sending thousands of fresh recruits off to die in a gruesome guerrilla conflict that was not well understood and not universally supported in the United States.

When Sonny graduated from high school, the U.S. was deploying its first combat units to the war. By the time he approached his college graduation from Indiana University, the country had approximately a half-million troops in Southeast Asia and had suffered nearly 50,000 deaths.

With the Vietnam War at its peak, the U.S. war machine needed a continuous supply of young men to put into helmets and foxholes. Military call-ups of college students were commonplace, but Sonny had managed to appeal two previous induction notices because he was still making passing grades in college. Once he graduated, however, he knew his number was up.

* * *

Goshen, Indiana, is the government seat of Elkhart County, and it was where Sonny's name was on a list, in a vault in a dark-paneled office in the County Courthouse. What the Selective Service did with this list was a secret more closely guarded than the formula for Coca Cola. Supposedly, every male registered for the draft when he turned 18, and the draft board decided whom to call to active duty based on a list ranked by birth date. The Pentagon would tell the draft boards how many warm bodies it needed, and the draft board would send out notices of congratulations to football players, stock boys, farm workers, all of whom were about to become elite killing machines.

The problem with the Selective Service was that it was more selective of some men than others. Once notified by the draft board, innovative men came down with incurable health problems, paid bribes and even disappeared to avoid the unpopular war. Political favors were called in, pressure was applied, and unbelievable hardship stories were invented. Occasionally a patriotic brave soul stepped forward and volunteered for service, providing another young man who didn't want to be killed in a Southeast Asian swamp with a few more months of trepidation before his name would ultimately be called.

In Elkhart County, the religious demographics presented an unusual situation for the Selective Service, as the county's population consisted of a large percentage of members of the Amish and Mennonite religions. Because of their faith, they steadfastly objected to serving in the military and claimed ineligibility based on conscientious objection. The draft board classified these men "CO," rather than the more common "1A" status that was given to luckless draftees shipped off to war.

For the 1A males in Elkhart County, the disproportionate number of Amish and Mennonite men in the population caused a real problem. When the Pentagon passed down the number of candidates they needed, the count was based on total population, giving no consideration to the throngs of conscientious objectors. So virtually every non-Amish 18-year-old man in Elkhart County with all his arms and legs and a minimal ability to see and speak would be drafted.

* * *

Sonny was not opposed to serving in the military. After all, his father had lived through the Big War, surviving the Battle of Coffee and Sugar Rationing at Camp Pendleton in war-torn California. Sonny knew his old man had it pretty good during WWII, stationed in the sunshine of the Golden State, working as an Army baker by day, going home to his wife in the evening and spending the weekends at the beach. So with his draft notice in hand he headed to the armed forces testing center in Indianapolis for a pre-induction physical. If he passed he would soon be called to active duty and assigned to one of the branches of the military. If he failed, he would head to Toledo, Ohio, to join Owens Corning's sales training school in the Glass Shaft, as the company's corporate headquarters was known.

* * *

Early on a Saturday, Sonny arrived at the predictably bland-looking testing center and took his place in the first of many long lines that he would stand in that day. Almost immediately, he and 200 other completely confused recruits were ushered into a large room commanded by a tall, humorless sergeant who seemed to have a personal grudge against everyone there. After two hours of IQ testing, they were all dismissed with a growl to move across the hall to another large room. Here the invited guests were commanded to strip to their underwear so a team of seemingly semi-skilled doctors could check every orifice and limb for abnormalities that might prevent them from killing Viet Cong.

The recruits toed a series of yellow lines taped on the floor, forming rows six deep. A medical officer in a white lab coat, clipboard in hand, addressed the group of nearly naked men with a grunt and instructed them to hold their arms over their heads. Then a team of enlisted Army medics came down the rows checking each candidate for abnormalities and communicable diseases.

Standing in the last row, Sonny glanced around the room and noticed a young man in the middle of the third row with only his left arm in the air. Thinking he was going to get his ass chewed off for not following instructions, Sonny realized the kid had only one arm. The visual startled Sonny as he thought, "How in the hell did this poor sap get this far?" When a medic reached the one-armed man, he was quickly pulled off the line and disappeared through a set of double doors at the far end of the room. Sonny never saw him again.

After getting a blood sample drawn, Sonny then came to a bored medic who took his blood pressure, filled out a short form and gave the report to an Army doctor sitting at a small table near the door. The equally bored doctor read each blood pressure chart before the recruit was dismissed from the room. The doc stopped the fellow in front of Sonny and said matter-of-factly, "Your blood pressure is too high. If you want out I can redline you right here." The poor fellow was caught off guard and didn't immediately answer. Impatient, the doctor sternly demanded, "Do you want to be in or out?" All the kid could do was stammer and mumble. "Okay then. You're in, asswipe, move on," the doctor said. Sonny watched this thinking, "Ask me. Please. Please ask me."

But he wasn't asked, and at the end of the day Sonny was informed he had a suitable IQ, wasn't missing any limbs, didn't have a communicable disease and was perfectly fit for work in a foxhole. This first-hand look at the military started Sonny thinking of becoming a malcontent.

Sonny notified Owens Corning he was probably going to be late for their sales training school — about two years late. The manager in charge of training said he would make a few calls around the Glass Shaft and see what he could do. Because the president of Owens Corning still had ties to the Pentagon, perhaps Gen. Norstad knew someone who knew someone who knew someone in the Pentagon who could help. But by the time that help was found, Sonny was already in the service.

* * *

A sympathetic grandma at the Elkhart County draft board who had taken a liking to the polite young IU graduate had tipped off Sonny that he was soon to receive a draft notice. To beat the Selective Service to the punch, he enlisted for a two-year hitch as an Army baker. But things didn't go as expected when he showed up for induction. Sonny was standing in a line with other recruits when a very tall, very dark and very intense-looking sergeant with a clipboard came walking down the line. The sergeant was so squared away he looked like he was made of concrete, and he would study a person in silence for a couple seconds before moving on. When he stopped at Sonny, he carefully looked him up and down and then asked how tall he was. A little puzzled, Sonny replied that he was 6 feet 2½ inches. With that the sergeant made a note on the paper attached to his clipboard and announced, "You're an MP." Sonny lodged a meek protest and tried to tell Sgt. Cement that he had made special arrangements to be a baker, but the sergeant gave him a look that could have killed a truckload of Viet Cong as he very slowly and deliberately repeated the words *"mil-it-ar-y po-lice-man"* before turning and walking away. Sonny was not a baker.

FIVE

Joe Holloway had blossomed since his Army days into a portly 248 pounds. And at 5 feet 7 inches, it was not a great look for him. He was too out of shape for manual labor and sweating like the fat man he was as he packed his well-used 1972 Ford Fairlane 500 with his old Army footlocker, a large cooler, several rifle cases and a large box of individual field rations called meals ready to eat, or MREs. Last, he loaded a couple mysterious duffle bags that were kept closeted away in the back of the garage. Joe, and occasionally Melissa, were the only ones allowed in the garage, but absolutely no one but Joe, including Melissa, ever saw the inside of the garage closet.

Melissa knew better than to ask Joe where he was going, but she didn't need to because she knew when

Joe packed the duffle bags that he would be playing war games in the bayou with that despicable Westwright character. She had told Joe what she thought of Lucas, once. According to police, her distrust had led to a major confrontation during which she had accidentally run into Joe's fist. Now she would be left at home without transportation. She hoped she had enough formula for their baby.

Joe was in a foul mood as he packed for his survivalist get-away weekend. Baby Kimberly was colicky and had cried much of the night, and Joe had not gotten up to help Melissa rock the newborn because that was "woman's work." Besides, it was her fault they had the kid in the first place. He had conveniently forgotten that Kimberly was conceived the night he came home dead drunk after trading shots and snorting cocaine with Lucas. He had violently attacked Melissa. It was all her fault.

* * *

Joe gunned the Fairlane down U.S. 90 toward Houma. Soon it was in his rear-view mirror as he pressed on toward Morgan City. Just outside town he stopped long enough to gas up, use the grimy restroom of the two-pump gas station, and grab a fresh bottle of vodka from the mom-and-pop liquor store across the street. Back on the highway he cut over to Route 182, which runs alongside a dense marsh. He turned off onto a marginally maintained parish two-lane road through a series of one-horse towns. After twenty minutes he exited the paved road onto a nondescript dirt road at a small weathered sign marked with a red X and drove about four miles down the heavily rutted path with mud holes big enough to house a hippo. The trail eventually ended at a padlocked wooden gate guarding the entrance into the Black Bayou. He opened the gate with his key and drove toward an opening in the trees.

* * *

The term "bayou" is original to Louisiana and believed to have come from the Native American word "bayuk," a word meaning "small stream." The term has come to mean the braided backwaters that are fed by the Mississippi River in the low-lying areas of Southern Louisiana. Here the marsh and wetland waters move very slowly and make an ideal habitat for creatures like alligators, crawfish, catfish and heavily armed survivalists. Joe felt at home in the bayou and for some strange reason found the hostile environment calming, almost comforting. Until he got roaring drunk.

Black Bayou, once a pristine stream, had become a polluted, log-jammed and overly sedimented swamp. Clogged with thick, sharp reeds and cypress trees with their root knees bending to reach above the high-water line, the bayou was home to corn snakes, venomous western cottonmouth pit vipers and speckled king snakes. Great blue herons and tall egrets skimmed the water lilies floating on the dark brown water, snapping up whatever they could grab.

Deep in this menacing wasteland was a military-style compound surrounded by triple strands of barbed wire. Inside the wire was a small village of six single-story structures, two made of heavy plywood and four fashioned from large steel shipping containers, the type that are loaded onto ocean freighters. The rotting wood buildings were wrapped in moss; the giant steel boxes were covered in thick orange rust. The buildings were randomly situated around a large fire pit lined with benches made from fallen cypress tress. The place looked like a dump.

As Joe pulled his car to a stop inside the compound, he could see that several other Brothers of the Red X had already arrived. He parked and began unloading his gear just as Lucas emerged from one of the shipping containers with a bottle of beer in one hand and a grenade in the other.

The Brothers of the Red X was a subversive group of radicals and misfits well-known to the nation's major law enforcement agencies, including the FBI; the U.S. Marshals Service; the Bureau of

Alcohol, Tobacco and Firearms; and the U.S. Drug Enforcement Agency. They were also on the radar of less well-known agencies such as the U.S. Postal Police, the IRS Criminal Investigation Division, and the Bureau of Engraving and Printing Police. Red X members also were being watched by numerous state and local police agencies, as well as various government departments and task forces.

The Brothers of the Red X network had formed in the late '60s as a splinter group made up of former members of the American Nazi Party, American Peace Crusade, Posse Comitatus and a few Republic of Texas dropouts. About a dozen other radical groups were represented in the hard-core membership that numbered just more than 150. Joe Holloway was a member in good standing.

Red X enterprises included gunrunning, selling stolen military ammo and drug sales. Their businesses had been profitable enough that the group was able to purchase a large tract of swampland in Black Bayou for their playground. Here they met on weekends to conduct business, blow things up and get drunk.

As darkness closed in on the swamp, Joe and Lucas finished off a bottle of Wild Turkey and snorted a couple lines of grade-A cocaine they had bought from an underworld Colombian contact. Joe was still in a dark mood, and it grew worse with each line of cocaine. He looked like a guy on a wanted poster at the post office, his face smeared with green, gray and black camouflage grease covering a three-day growth of beard. He had circles under close-set hazel eyes dulled by dope. He wore a tattered old Army field jacket over a flannel shirt and a pair of threadbare blue jeans. At Camp Red X he was a fashion plate.

Lucas tempted fate and cautiously spoke to Holloway. "Man, there's no moon tonight. The trail will be hard to find. Think we'll be able to locate my man out there?" Joe glared at Lucas for a minute and then answered in a slow, low mumble, "You had better find him, or you're a dead man." Lucas quickly decided not to press the conversation and went back to draining his bottle of bourbon and filling ammo clips.

* * *

A little after midnight, Joe and Lucas drove an all-terrain vehicle into the swamp about a half-mile from the compound. It was pitch dark in the swamp as the two-seater bounced along a narrow trail curving around clumps of cypress trees. Out of the blackness, a signal light flashed in the distance as they approached a small clearing. A few minutes later they were facing a sinister-looking Mexican standing next to a stack of wooden ammo crates. Without greeting the munitions salesman, Joe started inspecting the cache of bullets, and when satisfied with the quality, held up three fingers. The Mexican flashed a toothy grin of several gold-capped incisors and responded by holding up his left hand, wiggling five fingers. Joe frowned, thinking for a minute, and then showed four fingers. The Hispanic salesman laughed and shook his head to signal "no way." Joe took a step toward the Mexican; they were now just three feet apart. Lucas spoke up to break the tension, attempting to remind him that the previously agreed price was $3,000. But before he could complete a sentence, Joe had closed the distance to the Mexican and was holding an ominous-looking knife against his throat. The grin abruptly disappeared from the Mexican's face, and his hands shot up. Joe leaned in close and held up three fingers about an inch from the Mexican's nose. A quick nod signaled acceptance of the offer as a thin scarlet trickle of blood ran down the neck of the shaken and very wide-eyed Mexican.

A MOST DETERMINED LUNATIC

SIX

Sonny was contemplating enlisting in the Marine Corps and heading to Parris Island for boot camp when an aide to Gen. Norstad, the Owens Corning president, called at the eleventh hour and suggested Sonny pay a visit to an Army Reserve unit headquartered at Fort Benjamin Harrison.

Fort Ben, as it was known, was in Lawrence, Indiana, northeast of Indianapolis. Named for the 23rd president, the base housed the U.S. Army Finance School, the Interservice Postal School and the Defense Information School, and thousands of enlisted personnel and officers from various branches of the U.S. military staffed the schools. With all the training classes on post, the fort was sarcastically called "Uncle Ben's Rest Home," implying that no real military training took place there.

Also attached to Fort Ben was a company of Army Reservists designated as the 38th Military Police Company, a special unit of highly trained MPs attached to the 902nd Military Intelligence Group headquartered at Fort Benning, Georgia. The 902nd conducted counterintelligence for the Army and had its own police force. The Fort Harrison MPs were trained to be backups for the Fort Benning unit.

On a mild spring day in early May, Sonny drove through the main gate at Fort Benjamin Harrison on his way to an appointment with the non-commissioned officer in charge of the 38th Military Police Company. As he left his newly acquired red-and-white '64 Corvette, he could hear the faint whine of an Offenhauser racing engine on the track at the Indianapolis Motor Speedway across town. The city was gearing up for the Indy 500 on Memorial Day.

Cleared into the noncom's private office, Sonny was greeted by a 6-foot 4-inch hulk of a master sergeant in a crisp, highly starched and almost skin-tight MP uniform standing behind a large wooden desk. After Sonny had introduced himself, the master sergeant sat down in an old leather chair behind the desk, leaning as far back as possible, and thundered, "So, you're the kid who thought he was a baker."

A MOST DETERMINED LUNATIC

* * *

Sonny's military career was uneventful, despite the war festering in Southeast Asia. He was inducted into the Army and sent to a twelve-week basic-training program at Fort Campbell, Tennessee, where he joined more than a thousand other novice warriors. After mastering the art of bayoneting rubber mannequins and crawling under a series of wooden obstacles, Sonny was shipped off to Fort Gordon, Georgia, to the home of the Army's Provost Marshal School for Military Police. After three more months at the MP Academy honing his police skills, the Army said he was ready to go back to Indiana and protect Owens Corning Fiberglas.

Returning home twenty-two pounds lighter with a burr haircut, Sonny became a weekend warrior and joined the Owens Corning sales training class at the Glass Shaft in Toledo. Soon he was back in Indianapolis selling fiberglass insulation wholesale to major industrial accounts. His sales skills were solid, and he made good money, but the job didn't really appeal to him. He thought it was impressive that the company's business cards were printed on actual pieces of fiberglass, but he was having a hard time getting excited about selling insulation.

* * *

Joan Barton had also grown up in Elkhart County and also attended Goshen High School. Four years younger than Sonny, she had been a friend of his sister, who was in the same grade as Joan. Sonny knew Joan as a smart, cute and outgoing brunette who had been named Goshen's Junior Miss and had been in the queen's court during homecoming. After high school Joan had gone off to Ball State University a couple hours south of Goshen, but in two years she had grown weary of the teacher's college and the scene in Muncie. She transferred to the joint campus of Indiana University–Purdue University in Indianapolis and was accepted into the IU Nursing School.

Joan didn't have a car at college and in November found herself without a ride home for Thanksgiving. In hopes of saving her parents a five-hour round trip, she called Sonny to ask for a ride home. Sonny was glad to have company for the long drive but had forgotten most of what he had known about Joan. So he was pleasantly surprised to see the attractive co-ed come bounding down the steps as he pulled up to the Nursing School dorm.

Joan and Sonny hit it off right from the start, and soon they were seeing one another semi-regularly. After about six months, the arrangement became exclusive, but then Joan graduated with a degree in nursing and moved back to Goshen to work at the hospital.

* * *

After just two years with Owners Corning, Sonny had grown sufficiently bored with building supplies and insulation. He was tired of talking to lumber yard good ol' boys in overalls about the finer points of stuffing scratchy fiberglass into walls. So he contacted a recruiting firm and started looking at entry-level sales positions in the medical products industry. The field was heating up, and Sonny had heard there was big money to be made selling medical equipment. And though he interviewed with a couple small medical-supply companies, he didn't see much difference between selling fiberglass and Band-Aids.

But Sonny shined in an interview with a Johnson & Johnson headhunter, who encouraged him to pursue any available position with the company because it had a solid reputation as one of the best-run corporations in America and was seen as a first-rate training ground for those who desired to progress to a management career. So he quit Owens Corning and took a job with a new Johnson & Johnson subsidiary, Codman & Shurtleff, selling neurosurgical supplies and instruments to hospitals in the central Midwest. Mastering the company's diverse product line was challenging and required training classes that included watching real surgeries in person and scrubbing in on mock surgical procedures.

The training process was tough, and several new sales representatives disappeared from the training classes because they failed a test, or violated a corporate rule or wore the wrong color shirt while shadowing a sales trainer in the field.

The comprehensive education prepared him for the special trials of the job. Dealing with over-stressed surgical nurses, power-hungry hospital administrators and temperamental neurosurgeons made the job challenging, but he truly enjoyed selling a sophisticated product to highly educated and deeply motivated professionals. He mastered the technical product knowledge and became a good salesman at Codman, making the President's Sales Club in the first year. Soon, he was promoted to sales trainer, mentoring and evaluating new sales reps, the first step up the corporate ladder. The promotion meant more money in the short term and a career path for the long term. Sonny had found his niche in the business world and landed a job he was excited about.

* * *

The first rays of pale yellow sunlight were just beginning to break through the bedroom blinds in

Sonny's apartment as Joan eased out of bed. Sonny rolled over to watch her toned naked body glide effortlessly toward the bathroom. She was beautiful. Her long, dark hair fell gracefully across her deeply tanned shoulders and down her back. As she moved, her firm breasts bounced slightly with the rhythm of her stride. She had a slender waist and a nice tight behind. Joan had played field hockey at Ball State and still had the body of an athlete. Sonny let out a low whistle as Joan reached the bathroom. She turned and gave him a little smirk before disappearing through the doorway, allowing her leg to trail behind in her best showgirl impersonation. "You know, that kind of performance will only get you in trouble," Sonny teased.

"Give me fifteen minutes, and I'll show you some trouble," she shot back.

Joan emerged from the bathroom after a quick shower wrapped in a bath towel that didn't hide her femininity. Letting the towel fall to the floor, she slid back under the covers. Sonny rolled over and tenderly embraced her. She smelled of vanilla body lotion and tasted like peppermint. They made passionate love as the room filled with morning sunlight and then lay in each other's arms enjoying the moment.

Joan fell back to sleep, but Sonny's mind was working overtime.

Lately, Joan had been creeping to the front of Sonny's mind even when he tried not to concentrate on her. Could he be in love with her? He had never been in love before, despite having dated his share of suitable women. But deep in his heart, he knew Joan was different.

Joan was good-looking, smart and poised, and she was the only girl he knew who understood soccer's offside rule. She could keep a box score for a baseball game. Growing up with three older brothers, Joan had quickly learned how to hold her own while shooting hoops in the driveway. But Sonny didn't want to just play sports with her.

His thoughts shuffled through the current status of his life. Things were going well. He had a great job, drove an expensive car and had enough money to do what he wanted, when he wanted. He wasn't sure he wanted anything to change, yet he felt something was missing. Joan was everything he could ask for in a girlfriend. Until he had started dating her, he was content to look at relationships in the short term. But lately, he found that he had started thinking about the future — a lot. He was completely comfortable with Joan. He enjoyed being with her. Maybe it was time to make sure he didn't lose her.

Later, sitting in the kitchen's small breakfast nook, Sonny again watched Joan. She poured coffee and delivered two cups to the table. She noticed he was deep in thought and asked, "Hey babe, what's on that big business brain of yours this morning?"

Sonny was staring at the tabletop. He paused for a few seconds, then looked up and suddenly said, "I'm thinking we should get married."

Joan stopped in her tracks and slowly set the coffee cups on the table. To Sonny, time seemed to freeze until a small tear appeared in the corner of her eye and she eased down to sit in his lap. Joan gave him a long passionate kiss and whispered, "I'm thinking you're right, Mr. Corporate, but only if you promise to love me for the rest of my life."

Sonny stared into her eyes for a few seconds before tenderly whispering, "Lady, I can't promise that, but I will love you for the rest of *my* life."

They were married eight months later at the Methodist Church in Goshen. The twilight wedding was a beautiful candle-lit service with a reception at the Maple Creek County Club. Joan had left her job in Goshen to join Sonny in Indianapolis, so they were each starting new jobs. This mandated that the honeymoon be an abbreviated trip, and they left for Venice, Florida, for a few days of baking in the sun and splashing in the surf in the Gulf of Mexico. Venice was the winter home of the Ringling Bros. and Barnum & Bailey Circus so they attended a dress rehearsal that was open to the public. They visited the dog track and the historic Ringling mansion in

Sarasota, as well as Busch Gardens and the sprawling famous Kapok Tree restaurant in Tampa. They enjoyed each other day and night and were sad to bid the beach goodbye when they headed back to Indianapolis for work.

They returned to a new townhouse in the fast-growing and swanky suburb of Carmel, just north of Indianapolis. With a calico cat and a metallic gold Porsche 914, they were the all-American couple.

SEVEN

On March 14, 1973, Joe Holloway walked into the small suite on the eighteenth floor of the Downtown Howard Johnson Hotel in New Orleans' central business district precisely at 3 p.m. Two diminutive Japanese gentlemen in identical crumpled black suits and white shirts sat next to a big American man. The yank wore a Brooks Brothers navy-blue pinstriped suit and custom-made blue oxford button-down shirt. A small banquet table covered with a green tablecloth was positioned in front of the three executives. Joe was offered the only chair on the opposite side of the table.

A MOST DETERMINED LUNATIC

The American, Michael J. Opperman, had just
been named senior vice president of the new U.S.
Medical Instrument Division of Omniplex
Worldwide, a multi-billion-dollar international
imaging equipment conglomerate. Omniplex
manufactured a diverse product line of high-quality
surgical and scientific microscopes, optical testing
equipment, and both rigid and flexible fiber-optic
instruments used for industrial and surgical
applications.

Joe had been invited to interview for a sales
position with the start-up operation that would sell
Omniplex's line of revolutionary new fiber-optic
endoscopes in the United States. The scopes would be
manufactured in Japan but sold and serviced in the
United States by a direct sales force.

Endoscopes are diagnostic medical devices that
allow a physician to look inside the human body by
inserting a thin fiber-optic tube into the patient.
Various types of instruments had been used over the
years to look inside the human body; however,
Omniplex's devices were thinner, optically superior
and much more maneuverable than anything that had
previously been available. The scopes allowed doctors
basically to see inside a patient as though they were in
there themselves. Because they were better than
anything on the market, the endoscopes would be sold
at a premium price.

Endoscopes were the hot ticket in the medical device world in the late '70s, and Omniplex had the best ones available. To his very good fortune, Joe was talking to people who could make him a wealthy man. He put the skills he had learned from interviewing for multiple job changes to good use and walked away with a sales position far more lucrative than he could imagine.

* * *

Using skills he had honed selling pens and shelving, Joe quickly became a successful Omniplex endoscope salesman. Omniplex provided no sales training, but the product was so superior that even marginal representatives had no problem meeting their sales quotas. Those with some skill did well. And those with solid sales experience, like Joe, did very well. Almost everyone selling Omniplex endoscopes during this time became wealthy, as they were selling one of the most widely sought medical devices of the decade. At a list price of $4,000 to $10,000 per scope, Omniplex couldn't make the instruments fast enough, and they had no reason to discount the price.

As sales flowed in, Joe's commissions mounted; after just two years he was making almost $300,000 a year. He had always dreamed about having this type of disposable income but had never before come close to obtaining it. The money provided lots of luxuries that he and Melissa had never known. He bought a new car, then a second new car, then a new boat. Omniplex was pleased with Joe's performance and rewarded him with a larger territory that included all of Louisiana, Arkansas and Alabama, and most of Tennessee and Georgia. The money continued to roll in. In 1979, Joe was named Omniplex salesman of the year. He was on top of the world, as he had lucked into the job of a lifetime. The company gave Joe a big plaque and a diamond ring. What Omniplex didn't know was that he carried a switchblade in his pocket and a revolver in his briefcase and took a hit of cocaine before most sales calls.

Omniplex's commissions were so good during the early '80s that the freshly rich Holloways bought a half-acre corner lot in Destrehan, Louisiana, just off the Mississippi River, fifteen minutes west of New Orleans. Destrehan had been established in 1787 and was formerly the plantation home of Jean Noel Destrehan, who was appointed a U.S. senator when Louisiana became a state in 1812. Destrehan had a brief brush with national fame in 1974 when Gary Tyler, a black student, was accused by local officials of a tragic shooting. Tyler was convicted and sentenced to prison based on shaky testimony. Years later, Bob Herbert of the New York Times wrote about the story as "an egregious example of a racially motivated abuse of the justice system," and the residents of Destrehan still recoiled when visitors brought up the matter. But Joe knew the story and thought Gary Tyler got just what was coming to him.

* * *

Joe and Melissa's wooded lot was within walking distance of the Ormond Country Club near Cypress Lake. The club featured a large clubhouse framed by majestic cypress trees along a circular drive and offered tennis courts, a swimming pool and an 18-hole golf course. The Ormond neighborhood consisted of about 150 upscale homes worth up to $450,000. Joe contracted with a private builder to erect a lavish two-story brick home at 107 Villere Place on his half-acre backing the golf course. The four bedrooms, three bathrooms and three-car garage came complete with a nanny's quarters. The house had large bay windows downstairs and a spacious country-style kitchen. It had everything Joe had never wanted. To appease Melissa, he had approved the addition of many features he couldn't have cared less about. His interest centered almost solely on the garage and basement.

* * *

As the Destrehan house construction began, Joe made several last-minute design changes without telling Melissa. He ordered steel rebar rods sunk into the foundation that ran up through the window frames and door joists to strengthen them. Kicking your way into Joe's house would be difficult. He had the walls in the garage formed with multiple layers of concrete block so a vehicle couldn't plow through from the outside. Industrial steel shelving was placed in the third-car stall of the garage and bolted to the concrete floor so food and living supplies could be stored. He had several secret compartments built into the walls of the living quarters to hide guns and ammunition.

In the basement he made the most elaborate alterations. The foundation of the basement was poured double thick and extended above grade-level by a foot and a half. Every fifteen feet along the basement walls in the extended space small portholes were cut and covered with a thick steel plate that could be swiveled out of the way for a gun barrel. If you came to get him, Joe was planning on putting up a fight.

Joe's pride and joy, however, was the sub-basement, a small room several steps down from the main basement. The room was segregated from the rest of the basement by a heavy steel door with a peephole. In the center of this room was a workbench made from concrete blocks and topped with a solid cement slab. Openings were left in the concrete workbench supports for storing metal ammo cases and bullet manufacturing supplies. Mounted on the bench would be several pieces of equipment used to modify weapons. Here Joe would bore out gun barrels, customize pistol grips and convert semi-automatic assault rifles to fully automatic. Military-style metal gun racks would line the walls and be secured to the foundation. It was clear from the number of racks that would be installed that Joe was planning on storing a lot of guns.

With the new house complete, Joe went on a spending spree to fill all that storage space. For the garage, he bought crates of MRE food packets, cartons of canned goods, boxes of seeds, fifty-pound bags of flour and rice, equipment for distilling water, industrial-grade batteries and multiple hand-cranked radios and lights. He had almost everything a survivalist would need. To stock the basement bunker, however, he would need to go to Black Bayou.

* * *

The membership of the Brothers of the Red X gathered in the swamp about every six weeks or so when a meeting would be called by one of the fanatics to voice a real or perceived grievance, introduce a dope or munitions smuggler to the group, or stage a drunken party with an assortment of bar girls from Bourbon Street. With the house finished, Joe called Lucas and told him to spread the word that a meeting was needed; he wanted to acquire a cache of weapons and party with a couple of prostitutes.

A light drizzle was falling the day of the meeting. As dusk moved over Black Bayou, mud-splattered vans and pickup trucks started pulling into the compound. Lucas arrived in an old Ford Econoline van loaded with booze and several well-used hookers, and Joe arrived in his new Mercury with a bad attitude. High on amphetamines, by midnight he had bought more than $35,000 worth of guns, $2,000 of cocaine and the services of Raven LaMoore.

Raven was a French Quarter franchise, and like McDonald's had served thousands. She wore a long jet-black wig over her natural short mousy brown hair and a silk blouse unbuttoned almost to her waist. She had crammed her size 14 figure into a size 12 sequined pants suit, ideal for romping in the swamp. Raven's 38DD silicon breasts, which periodically popped out of her blouse, were her most valuable asset and were available for rent at a negotiated rate.

As their Red X brothers entertained the other van ladies around the fire pit, Lucas and Joe took Raven into one of the partially dilapidated buildings dubbed the "Hotel." While not up to Marriott standards, the

Hotel was cleaner than the other shacks and had relatively new mattresses and real sheets on the metal cots. The Hotel was a 15-foot-by-25-foot wood-framed structure with thick plywood walls and a tin roof. A wood-burning stove, a well-traveled credenza passing as a bar, and a string of trouble lights hanging from the ceiling completed the décor and established the Hotel's dubious ambiance.

Once inside, Joe's mood changed from dark to black. He sniffed long lines of cocaine and followed each hit with a shot of vodka. Soon he was completely plastered. He sat at a small table repeatedly sticking his switchblade into the wood while staring at Raven. Lucas was discussing a business arrangement with Raven when suddenly Joe charged him and grabbed him by the throat. Lucas went limp as Joe walked him to the door and threw him outside. With Lucas gone, he turned his attention to Raven. She had seen gentlemen joust for her affection before so she was not overly concerned until Holloway forcefully grabbed her.

Joe pushed Raven into a corner and shredded her blouse, manhandling her breasts and fondling her crotch. Next he ripped off her slacks and forced her to her knees. Raven started to resist, but a fist to the temple knocked her into compliance. Joe dropped his pants and thrust his manhood into her face. Raven submitted, thinking this would satisfy him, but she significantly misjudged the situation.

The next thing Raven felt was her left arm exploding in pain. Joe had run the blade of his knife along her bicep, and bright red blood oozed from the cut and dripped from her elbow. Before Raven could yell out, another blow to the head sent her sprawling on the floor. Joe pounced on her and dragged her to a nearby cot, where he repeatedly used the unconscious prostitute to please himself.

Lucas may not have been a rocket scientist, but he was smart enough to know not to re-enter the Hotel while Joe and Raven were "partying." After an hour and a half, Joe emerged from the Hotel, and Lucas asked, "If you're finally finished with the young lady, I'd like to spend a little time with her?" Joe didn't look at him but snarled as he walked away from the door, "She's done for the night, asshole." This didn't compute for Lucas: She was a hooker, and he had money, so he started into the Hotel to try to talk Raven into reconsidering. As Lucas passed Brother Joe, Holloway pulled a snub-nosed .38 out of his back pocket and planted it squarely in the middle of Lucas's chest. "Did you not hear me say that she isn't interested, shit brain?" Joe growled. "Or do I need to use this on you to get you to take a hike?" With that, Joe punched Lucas in the chest hard with the nose of the pistol, and Lucas shot his arms up over his head and quickly backed away.

The Red X shindig came to a drunken end around 3 a.m., and one by one the comrades drove out of the compound. Lucas waited in the van for Raven to leave the Hotel, but Joe told him that he would drive her back to Bourbon Street. So Lucas loaded the remainder of his well-sampled cargo back into the Econoline and headed for the highway. Holloway was the last to leave. About 4 a.m. he departed the compound heading for New Orleans. He was alone.

A MOST DETERMINED LUNATIC

EIGHT

Sonny and Joan enjoyed their new life together. They worked hard through the day and made love at night. Joan was a nurse at a busy regional hospital, and Sonny traveled throughout the Midwest peddling neurosurgical equipment. Their combined incomes let them live comfortably and take an occasional vacation.

Sonny practiced keeping America free by attending Army Reserve drills one weekend a month with his Military Police company at Fort Benjamin Harrison. Several times a year, the unit held special field training at Camp Atterbury, about 45 minutes south of Indianapolis. The installation, built during the 1940s on 40,000 acres of forestland, contained more than a thousand vacant wooden buildings. The guys in Sonny's unit called it Camp Mayberry, after the Andy Griffith Show, because the buildings gave the illusion of a small town. When one of the MP's did something stupid he would be called a "Barney," after Mayberry's bumbling deputy sheriff Barney Fife.

Herds of deer roamed the Atterbury grounds, and twice a year the state opened the post to specially permitted hunters to thin the herd. A large portion of the land was used as a target range for Air Force bombing runs and was off-limits to everyone. The base was used during World War II to house German and Italian prisoners of war and later as a training base for the Indiana National Guard. By special agreement with Indiana, the Army sent Sonny's MP unit to Camp Mayberry once a quarter to train to control riots and civil disturbances. The vacant wooden structures were perfect props to use for police training.

Sonny liked being an MP and for a while toyed with leaving the medical-products industry to become an officer with the Indiana State Police. He never made the move, but occasionally he would ride along with one of his MP buddies during their regular police shifts.

Sonny moved up through the ranks from private to specialist to sergeant. After the most recent promotion, he became a staff sergeant leading the company's riot-control platoon. He attended special classes and received intense field training necessitated by the significant amount of civil unrest in the country in the late '60s and early '70s, as there was an undercurrent of discontent in the country caused by the war in Asia. Sonny was attending an Army class on crowd control the evening of the Kent State massacre, when the Ohio National Guard fired on a group of unarmed students who were protesting the war, killing four and wounding nine.

This was Sonny's worst nightmare about being an MP. He could live with his car being egged at night while parked outside the townhouse or being called "pig" by college students when he stopped to get gas while in uniform. His fear was being the leader of a bunch of 19- and 20-year-old gun-happy reservists called to put down a major student disturbance. He had little concern about his ability to handle such a situation but was terrified that one of his charges would panic, disregard orders and fire into a group of civilians. So Sonny made sure that a couple of the platoon's "Barneys" never had loaded weapons and were kept as far away from the action as possible.

Some time later, Sonny put his training to use when in 1974 his MP company was activated to assist the Indiana State Police after a disastrous tornado tore through Michigan City, Indiana. The situation overwhelmed the local police and state troopers, as all the power and phone lines were down, roads were closed, and emergency services were strained to the breaking point. Sonny's MP company provided traffic control, armed security patrols, criminal investigations and temporary jail facilities, working twelve-hour shifts patrolling the streets to give the local police a breather.

* * *

The headhunter on the phone was looking for talent for a new division of Omniplex Worldwide. Sonny was content working for Johnson & Johnson and had a bright future there, but he became more interested as the recruiter outlined the possibilities.

This sales position was with a high-tech medical device company and would put him in the big leagues. He was open to taking a peek at the opportunity.

In medical products sales there was a hierarchy of importance, which translated to an increase in pay. To arrive at a top-tier company that paid their sales representatives top dollar, a candidate usually had to move up the ranks of the medical-products industry. A career-motivated man could move up within a specific company and obtain a higher pay grade, but the starting pay of a company on the next tier up often paid almost as much as a mid-level position on the tier below.

The first tier on the medical sales ladder was occupied by pharmaceutical sales. Drug reps were generally the lowest paid and the most highly managed sales people. Next came the disposable medical supply industry. Direct sales reps and distributors for companies in this tier sold bandages and crutches, sutures, patient gowns, surgical scrubs and other disposable hospital necessities. The third level was the non-disposable supply business. Salesmen in this tier sold reusable supplies and low-cost hospital equipment such as X-ray film trays, stethoscopes, doctors' headlamps and suction pumps.

At the fourth tier, companies carried implants, medical instruments and capital equipment — in other words, big-ticket budget items. Sonny had managed to skip the first three levels of the medical sales ladder and had started in this tier with Codman & Shurtleff. Now a recruiter was calling him about a move to the top tier. This level was the home of the highest-priced instrumentation and specialty surgical equipment and the best-paid medical sales reps. At the top of the heap were the guys selling high-tech medical equipment such as lasers, magnetic resonance imaging units and flexible fiber-optic endoscopes.

* * *

Sonny gave the headhunter the information he needed and clearance to put his name in play with Omniplex, and less than 24 hours later a preliminary interview was arranged with Mark Tyler, Omniplex's 44-year-old national sales manager. Tyler looked like a GQ model: tall and thin, dark-haired, good-looking, well-dressed. The ladies noticed this, and he was chronically on the prowl. He grew up in Kansas City, played tennis at a Jesuit high school and earned a business degree from Kansas State University, where he met and married his wife. Tyler had worked his way up through the medical equipment industry and was one of the first salesmen Mike Opperman had hired when Omniplex opened its U.S. endoscope division. Tyler was now hiring the second wave of sales reps.

Sonny flew to Chicago and met Tyler during the lunch hour at an Omniplex branch office near O'Hare International Airport. He was impressed that the company had sent a limo to pick him up. The interview at the branch office was held while Tyler ate a Cobb salad at a borrowed desk. The meeting was quick and direct, and there was no small talk. Tyler offered Sonny nothing to eat or drink and gave no indication how he had fared during their discussion. By early afternoon, Sonny was back in the limo headed for the airport. Once he was home, Joan asked how the interview went. "I think I blew it," Sonny said. "The man was cold as ice and hardly asked me any questions. They flew me all the way to Chicago to watch the guy eat his lunch." He was fairly certain Tyler hated him.

Two days later, Sonny answered the phone to find he had been wrong. Tyler was inviting him to fly to Omniplex corporate headquarters in Jericho, New York, to talk about working for the company. The recruiter told Sonny the job was his to lose, saying he would know how he stood if he got to meet anyone more senior than Tyler at Omniplex during his visit.

Sonny arrived in the morning at the American Airlines terminal at New York's LaGuardia Airport in Queens. The airport was a dump and nearly deserted, even at peak arrival time. The corridors were dirty; many shops were out of business, and the airport staff was surly at best. Several men who looked homeless appeared to have set up housekeeping on benches near baggage claim, where dozens of limo and cab drivers accosted arriving passengers with offers of off-the-meter discounted rides into the city.

Among pilots, LaGuardia was referred to as "USS LaGuardia" because the runways were extremely short and built out over Flushing Bay, giving the slightly scary feeling of touching down on an aircraft carrier. This was Sonny's first impression of New

York City, and he overcame the urge to get right back on a plane and head home.

A Lincoln Town Car awaited Sonny just outside baggage claim and swept him to Jericho. The corporate office was underwhelming. The company was in a large old corporate office complex of identical off-white buildings. The narrow driveways dividing the complex into sections were lined with incredibly tight parking spaces, and it looked to Sonny as if a driver would have to jump out of his moving car aimed into a parking spot and let it roll into the space because there wasn't room to open the door once parked.

After he was dumped in the parking lot, Sonny entered Building 2-B through a nondescript set of double doors and found the inside of the building equally uninspiring. There was no lobby, just a metal staircase leading from the small entry to a metal door on the second floor. Sonny climbed the stairs and upon opening the door walked directly out into a cubical village. At least fifty work stations were in the center of the floor with a series of small offices lining the windowed outside walls. The dull brown carpet was threadbare and patched in several places with silver duct tape. No art was on the walls, and the lighting was only slightly better than working by candlelight. The overall decor was Early Goodwill. A young lady at one of the gray metal desks near the door looked up and with typical New York hospitality growled, "What do you want?" Sonny said he had flown in from Indianapolis for a meeting with Mark Tyler. The woman frowned and asked, "Indianapolis, is that where all the Navy people are?" At first Sonny was puzzled but then realized she was thinking of Annapolis, the U.S. Naval Academy, in Maryland. With a smile Sonny said, "No, Indianapolis is the capital of Indiana." The woman pondered this for a couple seconds and then ended the conversation with the mystifying statement, "Oh yeah, in Ohio." Under his breath Sonny muttered, "So much for welcome to the Big Apple."

Mark Tyler's office was an eight-foot-by-eight-foot box with old furniture and a wheezing steam radiator. The window was cracked open despite the snow flurries outside because it was about 90 degrees in the room. His office door just cleared a wooden armchair in front of the small desk. Sonny took a seat across from Tyler.

After a brief meeting with the national sales manager, Sonny was ushered to the corner office of Michael Opperman, the recently promoted president of the Medical Equipment Division. His office was much larger and brighter, had windows on two sides, and was big enough for an executive desk and two leather armchairs. In the corner was a small round conference table with four chairs. Opperman, wearing a new custom-made white button-down shirt with the sleeves rolled up, navy-blue suspenders and an expensive bold designer tie, looked every bit the part of a busy successful corporate executive. He was sitting behind his large mahogany desk but quickly rose to meet Sonny halfway across the room. They sat at the conference table and talked for almost forty-five minutes. Opperman, who already knew all about Sonny's sales career, asked about his family, hobbies and career aspirations. Unlike Tyler, Opperman smiled at Sonny when he spoke and acted genuinely interested in what he was saying.

The conversation was casual, pleasant and informative but ended when a short, bald gentleman entered the room. Opperman introduced him as Sidney Korman, president of Omniplex U.S. Korman wore an expensive Hickey Freeman gray pin-striped suit, a white-on-white silk shirt, a bland navy-blue tie and black Florsheim Imperial wingtips with a shine so polished Sonny could see the overhead lights reflecting on the toes. He spoke briefly to Sonny in a heavy New York accent evangelizing on the many virtues of Omniplex. Minutes later without saying goodbye, Korman wheeled around and left the room. Sonny quickly concluded that he would be one of the little people who occasionally stumbled into Korman's corporate world, with whom the president tried to have as little interaction as possible.

On the plane ride home Sonny rewound the meetings in his mind. He felt he had a shot at the job but questioned whether he wanted it. The home office was a wreck, the staff was rude, the big boss was devoid of personality, and he did not care much for New York.

When Sonny arrived home, Joan could hardly wait for him to drop his overnight bag in the entryway to ask, "Well, how did the interview go?" Sonny frowned and told Joan, "I'm pretty sure I will get an offer, but I've decided not to accept the job, assuming it's offered. I'm on a good career path now with a stable company and make good money at Johnson and Johnson. Besides, I wasn't all that impressed with some of the people in the home office." He didn't say anything to Joan about his other big doubt, but he was concerned about working for a Japanese-owned company. He didn't know specific negatives, but he just had a general uneasiness about staking a career move on a foreign company. Joan sensed there was more to be told but decided to let the topic drop until Sonny felt like letting her in on the rest of the story.

Then the phone rang, and Mark Tyler offered Sonny a position selling endoscopes in the vacant Michigan-based territory. The conversation was short and to the point. Sonny hung up the phone and announced to Joan that he was the new Michigan Omniplex sales rep, the twenty-second employee of the endoscope division. Joan gave Sonny a look that shouted, "What the...?" Sonny simply shrugged and said, "It's more than double the pay."

* * *

The Grahams bought a two-story, 2,800-square-foot home being built in the Independence Hills subdivision in Farmington Hills, Michigan. They paid $145,000 for the house on a heavily wooded lot on the highest elevation in Oakland County. The house at 25286 Witherspoon Road overlooked a 300-acre nature park owned by the family of one of the city's founders. Farmington Hills was the second-largest city in the county and an upscale northwestern suburb of Detroit. However, Sonny and Joan's home was only twenty-four miles northeast of downtown Ann Arbor and the University of Michigan campus, both of which were closer than the business district of Detroit. Sonny and Joan had selected Farmington Hills because the picturesque beauty of the hilly landscape was unmatched in the Detroit area. Also high on the list were Farmington Hills' excellent schools, quaint downtown shopping district and its routine ranking as one of the safest cities in the United States.

Sonny's sales territory comprised all of Michigan, plus the northern part of Ohio. The business of flexible fiber-optic endoscopy was booming, and soon he was driving a new gray Mercedes Benz 300D sedan, which was probably not the most endearing car to drive in the heart of the U.S. auto industry. That was made clear to him one afternoon when he called on an ancient sprawling General Motors plant in the oldest industrial area of Detroit.

The United Auto Workers union had been battling with GM for years for additional health benefits they wanted in their contract with the automaker. As a negotiating tool, the union had focused on the rate of colon cancer among the model makers in the GM design center. The model makers turned drawings of futuristic automobiles into full-scale models made from clay and balsa wood, and the craftsmen were continually exposed to airborne dust particles, which recently had been linked to elevated occurrences of colon cancer.

The union had won an agreement for GM to provide free sigmoidoscopy screening for everyone who worked in the design center, and these procedures would be performed in GM's own care units in production facilities around the country. A sigmoidoscopy was a procedure performed with a flexible endoscope to examine for colon cancer. After protracted negotiations with GM's corporate purchasing department, Sonny sold GM two complete Omniplex sigmoidoscopy sets for every one of their medical facilities in the United States. The downside of the agreement was that Sonny had to personally deliver the equipment to the facilities in his territory to make sure the staff doctors and nurses knew how to care for it.

While visiting the massive Hamtramck Assembly Plant on the edge of Detroit, he encountered a gruff security guard at the main gate. Sonny needed to drive to the medical unit below street level in the bowels of the expansive production facility to unload equipment, but the gate guard would give him clearance for the car only as far as the employee parking lot. He parked his Benz in a sea of Chevys and Buicks and went about the chore of trucking the medical equipment a half-mile across the complex to the medical center on a hand cart. When he returned to his car a couple hours later, he found a large crowbar sticking through the windshield. Unfortunately for Sonny, the group of union members standing nearby all turned out to be completely blind and had no idea what had happened.

* * *

Sonny quickly became an accomplished endoscope salesman. In 1979 and then again in '80 he led the Midwestern Region in sales. This accomplishment was exceptional given that in the early '80s the U.S auto industry was beginning to experience serious problems. Problems at Ford and GM meant problems for Michigan as the impact of foreign imports on the car market rippled down from large parts suppliers to small accessory providers. As the supplier network came under distress, autoworkers started losing their jobs, which caused a major slowdown in the state's economy. Plans for new hospitals and expansion of existing medical facilities were cancelled, and many specialty medical practices closed. Graduating gastroenterology doctors who would normally be purchasing complete endoscopy sets for their new practices routinely elected to move out of state.

While most sales territories in the southern and western United States were experiencing an exponentially expanding need for equipment as a result of population shift, Sonny was dealing with hospital closures and a shrinking population base. However, even given the stale economy in 1982, he ranked second in the nation in total sales revenue for the Medical Products Division.

In 1981, the company's annual awards retreat was held for salesmen and their wives at the Princess Hotel in Acapulco. Omniplex flew more than 100 people to Mexico for the celebration, and Sonny and Joan enjoyed four days in the sun and surf hobnobbing with company bigwigs and other top sales producers. Omniplex was earning money hand over fist, so no expense was spared in making their VIP sales team feel appreciated. The company picked up expenses for rooms, meals, sightseeing, parasailing, deep-sea fishing, golf and other recreational events. The wives went shopping while their ultra-competitive sales warriors played golf and tennis for high-stakes cash. The last night in Mexico the company hosted a formal awards dinner in the hotel's main ballroom.

The men wore suits, and the ladies were decked out in fine dinner dresses. The lights were low, and a trio played softly in the corner of the ballroom. Round tables for ten covered with black tablecloths and sparkling white china were situated around the room and decorated with flowers and candles. As each couple entered the room through a floral arch, the wife was presented with a gift-wrapped blue box containing a small Tiffany sterling-silver bud vase. Omniplex was not above a little bribery to ensure the spouses were totally on board.

After dinner Michael Opperman addressed the gathering, a large screen with the company logo ten feet high behind him. Displaying his usual charm and quick wit, Opperman gave a short overview of the past year's accomplishments and talked briefly about plans for future growth. His speech was informative but lighthearted and just long enough to make everyone feel important but short enough not to be boring. When he finished, he introduced Mark Tyler, who would present the winners of the sales awards.

Tyler lacked the charm of Opperman and often came off as condescending. He was sharp, but calculating, and noticeably self-centered. He wasn't about to let anyone get around him during his quest for the corner office, even if his adversary were more talented. He gave a brief speech highlighting his own achievements, then passed out the regional sales awards. More than once his comments about the winner seemed to be a back-handed compliment. Sonny was surprised but not really upset when his name was not called. He felt he had turned in a record performance and expected to win the regional sales award again. Regardless where he finished, he had the commission money so he would let the oversight slide.

As the achievement parade drew to a close it was time to hand out the top award. Tyler started droning on about the accomplishments of the winner without stating his name. After a couple minutes, Sonny noticed Joan intently looking at him, and then he realized Tyler was talking about him. At that point he became a bit self-conscious. Tyler called Sonny to the stage and presented him with a large brass plaque, reading the inscription to the audience as Sonny stood uncomfortably at his side.

OMNIPLEX WORLDWIDE CORPORATION

Presented for the Year
1981

**to Sawyer R. Graham
SALESMAN OF THE YEAR**

Sonny accepted the award, shook hands with Tyler and Opperman and acknowledged the applause of the audience. He returned to his seat and gave Joan a kiss on the cheek as Opperman declared the event closed. As was the tradition of the event, the past winners of the Salesman of the Year Award lined up and filed by Sonny to offer congratulations. All the past winners except one. Joe Holloway stared at the flower arrangement in the center of his table, too intoxicated to move.

When they returned to their room a little after midnight, Joan poured Sonny a glass of wine and said she too had a surprise for him. She crossed the room with his wine and a glass of club soda for herself, raising her glass and offering a toast to the new father-to-be.

NINE

Sonny's climb up the Omniplex sales pyramid started with a phone call from Mark Tyler's gatekeeper, Kelly Upton. Kelly was a petite dark-haired cheerleader type who had been hired for the secretarial pool when Omniplex opened its U.S. offices. When Mark Tyler became national sales manager, she became his private secretary, and when Tyler was promoted, Kelly moved up with him, ranking as a senior administrative assistant.

Kelly was Tyler's first line of defense and had his back at all times. Tyler had become vice president of sales of the Medical Products Division and a busy man, far too busy to dial a number and wait for the phone to ring. Kelly handled all these mundane duties, and getting through her to get to him was not an easy task. Kelly protected Tyler with an iron fist and a typical New Yorker's moxie. In return for policing his domain, reporting back on anything she learned of substance and getting rid of anything he didn't want seen, Tyler had an ongoing affair with her that she believed was based on true love.

Kelly called Sonny one day and told him to catch an afternoon plane to New York the following day. He would have dinner with Tyler and be booked into a hotel overnight, but she told him to leave his return flight open. The call was a mystery to Sonny. He had no fear he was being summoned to be fired, as his sales record was one of the best in the company. However, he had no idea what Tyler wanted. Kelly's thinly veiled claim of ignorance left Sonny even more perplexed because he knew that she knew what was in store for him.

Tyler was almost friendly during the dinner. The conversation was polite and centered on himself. He never inquired about Joan or asked Sonny any personal questions, and during a dessert of cheesecake, he arrived at the reason for the meeting. Swearing Sonny to secrecy, Tyler told him he was considering a management change in the Southwest Region. The entire sales, service and administrative operation headquartered in Houston was underperforming. Sales were booming across the country, but they were lagging in the mid-South. The service center was a mess, and administrative costs were out of hand. Tyler was considering offering Sonny the chance to move to Houston and take control of the situation. Sonny was surprised and flattered; he didn't envision Tyler as his champion. He told Mark he was extremely interested in the challenge but would want to talk to Joan before committing to it. Tyler seemed bemused by this; it never would have occurred to him to discuss anything like this with his own wife. He responded by saying he wanted to move quickly to plug the leak so Sonny would need to make a decision as soon as possible.

The next morning Sonny met Tyler in Mike Opperman's office, and it quickly became clear that Opperman was the one who picked Sonny for the job. Opperman put his take on the opportunity and told Sonny not to rush a decision. He advised Sonny to go home, talk to Joan and take a couple days to think about it. Tyler was peeved that his power play had been pre-empted and that he had not played his cards more forcefully, but he said nothing.

* * *

On the flight back to Michigan, Sonny was absorbed in thought about the significant challenge he had been offered. A promotion to Houston might be a suicide mission. The Southwest sales region was a train wreck. The sales force was a motley crew of underachieving old-timers hired by the Japanese. The region's two service centers in Houston and Memphis were dumps managed by a former customer service clerk who ran them as if she were a sorority's aging house mother.

Then there was the issue of the move. Joan had quit her nursing job to stay at home with their daughter, Wren. The move might prove traumatic to the 3-year-old, and Joan would have no support group in Houston. And then there was the issue of selling their home. The economy in Michigan was hurting because of the major downturn of the auto industry, and the housing market in the Detroit area was fast moving toward free-fall. Last, Sonny thought about how the new job would affect his relationship with Joan. He would be traveling a lot, and Joan would be left alone to deal with broken water heaters, dead car batteries and ants marching through the kitchen. He was concerned she might not support his interest in the opportunity.

Sonny dropped his overnight bag in the entryway and kissed his wife and daughter hello. As had become a standing tradition when he traveled, he presented Wren with a stuffed animal he had purchased for her in New York. A furry lion named Leo would join the other plush critters on the shelves that lined Wren's bedroom, a hundred fuzzy friends watching over the little girl as she slept.

Joan was curious why Sonny had been summoned to the corporate office and was quick to broach the subject: "Okay, Mr. Corporate, what did Tyler want with his star performer that a phone call couldn't handle?" Sonny relayed the high points of the conversation and explained that the promotion offer had been dangled like a carrot hanging from a big stick. "There are some real negatives in the deal, but overall it is a major opportunity," Sonny said. "I would be the youngest regional manager in the company's history and have responsibility for about one-sixth of the division's total sales revenue. I know I can make a difference, but it requires a move to Houston." Sonny let the last statement hang in the air a bit before asking, "Well, what do you think?"

Sonny was pleased that Joan was on board with the move from the start. She supported him and knew he was the right man for the job. She would miss her dear friends but could keep in touch with them and make new ones in Houston. Wren was so young they reasoned she would survive any short-term distress. There was, however, real concern about selling the house. Homes in their immediate area were selling faster than in most of southeastern Michigan, but that was not saying much. They feared they might take a 30 to 40 percent loss on their property. After talking to a real estate agent, there was good news: They might lose only 20 percent.

* * *

Sonny called Mark Tyler to discuss the Houston opportunity. He wanted to accept the promotion but needed to lock down the details. Would Omniplex help with the move? Tyler said the company would pay for the relocation cost, help with sale of the house and provide a cost-of-housing salary adjustment. Would he have a free hand to deal with the problem senior sales people? Tyler lied and said he would. Sonny wanted assurance that he would be able to realign the Houston branch office as a first priority. Again Tyler lied his confirmation. Sonny moved on to discuss his compensation, but Tyler skillfully zigzagged through the topic without committing to much of anything. After serious negotiations, Tyler begrudgingly offered a modest raise, pledged that within reason expense money would not be a problem for travel, and agreed that the company would pick up the cost of temporary housing in Houston until the Grahams bought a new home.

After playing cat-and-mouse with Tyler for an hour it became clear to Sonny he would have to accept the job based on the routine concessions he had already won. He aborted further negotiations on additional big-ticket items such as increasing the regional commission overrides and bonuses, and accepted the position as offered. He would try to weasel additional concessions out of Tyler after he had proved himself in the job. Tyler wanted him in Houston as soon as possible so Sonny decided to commute to Houston until he could get a fair price for their house.

* * *

On the flight to Houston for his first meeting with the Southwest sales force, Sonny reviewed his deployment strategy and the troops he had at his disposal. His options were limited.

Bob Felton from the south side of Houston was a bumbling farm boy who raised show rabbits and spent more time at state fairs with his bunnies than he did selling endoscopes. Bob was a sloppy dresser, a slow thinker and always disorganized. He also was a devoted Christian and a nice guy adrift in the wrong profession.

Al Fishman covered Dallas and would have preferred to be his son's full-time soccer coach. He gave Omniplex almost 100 percent of the work day he had left after coaching soccer.

John Rosenthal from Kansas City was a total party animal. Already on his third marriage, he was continually on the prowl for a new conquest, and his ability to arrive at company meetings direct from all night sales calls on nurses was legendary.

Then came Richard Waltz, a pleasant loser from San Antonio who simply could not get things right. A constant worrier and chronic insomniac, Dick spent most of his time drinking large quantities of black coffee and concocting alibis to explain his poor sales results.

Roger Cenler was a potential keeper. He had done reasonably well in the field but was no dynamo. He had been in the first field sales group hired by the Japanese when Omniplex had brought their endoscopes to the U.S. He was a decent salesman but a poor manager and for some unknown reason had been promoted to national sales manager before Tyler had taken control. Roger had worked his way back down the corporate ladder and now was a salesman on the north side of Houston.

The only bright bulb in the box was Jimmy Shipman. Working out of Memphis, Jimmy was a self-motivated steady performer who could be counted on in a pinch, and he was the reason the Memphis branch office was in better shape than the main office in Houston. Sonny knew he could trust Jimmy to protect his back if things started to swing out of control.

And then there was Joe Holloway.

By this time, Joe was a member of the Million Dollar Roundtable for having amassed total career sales of over $10 million. Lately, however, his sales achievements had been subpar at best, and complaints were mounting by the day. Sonny had watched Joe from afar at company meetings and did not like what he saw. Joe was non-communicative, sullen, aloof and frankly a bit scary. There were rumors that he always carried a knife and slept with a revolver under his pillow.

Sonny recalled the company's last national sales meeting that had been held at the beautiful 600-room Phoenician Resort at the base of Camelback Mountain in Scottsdale, Arizona. It had been an elaborate affair of fine dining, golf and tennis, with some business thrown in for good measure. The major business meetings that everyone attended were staged in the main ballroom, but small breakout groups met outside on the greenbelts surrounding the championship golf course. Banquet chairs, flip charts and coffee services were placed at each location. The sales force had been divided into small clusters, each assigned to start at a different location. The plan was that the groups would rotate every 45 minutes to the next session in the circle so that by the end of the morning everyone would have visited all the stations and each salesman would have attended all the different discussions related to Omniplex's product line.

Sonny recalled seeing Holloway dressed in total black —slacks, shirt, sports coat, even aviator sunglasses — sitting ramrod straight in the front row of the first breakout group. On his way back to the main building for lunch, Sonny recalled seeing Joe still sitting straight as a board in the same seat in the same breakout location where he had started. At lunch Sonny asked the moderator of the first breakout session about Joe and was told that Holloway hadn't moved all morning. Concerned that Joe might be dead, the moderator had checked him in the second hour, finding him breathing but unconscious. Joe was in an alcoholic stupor so he had been left sitting in the chair when the last group broke for lunch.

TEN

Sonny realized that managing the Bad News Bears of the Southwest Region would be difficult, but he had a master plan. He would set specific obtainable goals for the region as a whole, as well as for each sales territory. These regional objectives would be in addition to the simple quota numbers passed down from Mark Tyler's office in Jericho.

Tyler's numbers tracked basic revenue. Sonny's objectives would focus on gross margin profit: He would push his troops to sell the equipment that made the company the most money. He would then closely monitor each rep's progress, praising and rewarding the ones obtaining positive results and consoling those falling short of their objectives. His end game was that he would quietly begin shopping for new talent because he knew several of his charges would never make the grade.

Sonny had wanted to part company with several of the losers immediately; however, Mark Tyler reneged on his pledge to give him a free hand and refused to allow any terminations. Tyler was concerned he might look bad in the eyes of the Japanese, who were reluctant to fire anyone, no matter how egregious their transgressions.

Sonny countered by realigning the entire region so he could create new territories. He hired four young studs who had previously demonstrated their sales prowess at lower levels in the medical products industry.

Ernie Tanner had sold for U.S. Surgical and got a territory in Oklahoma City. Lloyd Hoyt was a Mississippi State grad and son of the old South. He was awarded a new slot in Jackson. David DeVoss was a Dallas native with a strong medical supply background at American Hospital Supply. Last hired was the most promising of the lot, Jay Draper. A former semi-pro baseball player, Jay was a handsome blond with a pleasant personality and a smooth, polished sales style. He also had been a big hitter at American Hospital Supply and had covered most of Louisiana. Jay received Arkansas and northern

Louisiana, part of Joe's old territory, and was a welcome relief to Joe's long-suffering customers. Sonny's new steeds broke from the gate in a full gallop and soon were running rings around the rest of the pack. In six months, Sonny had the region running in high gear, though not without a few casualties.

First to go was "Bunny" Bob Felton. He made the mistake of disappearing from work for two weeks to show his rabbits at the Texas State Fair without telling Sonny he would be gone or asking for vacation time. When he finally showed up again for work he asked for a raise, even though he was the worst in the region by a long way at meeting his quota. Bob walked into Sonny's office in the Houston branch one day and announced that he needed more territory so he could make more money. Sonny pointed out that if he worked five days a week he would make more money. Felton then shot himself in the foot with the ultimatum that if he did not get his old territory restored he would resign. Sonny calmly told Bob that he accepted his resignation. Bob was stunned and asked if he had just quit. Sonny replied, "Yes, you did."

Next to go was Al "Soccer" Fishman. He was a wormy, chain-smoking man who was starting to fold under the pressure of being asked to do his job. He took his son's soccer team to a weeklong tournament in California without declaring the trip as a vacation or telling Sonny he would be gone from his sales territory. While he was out of state, there was a major problem at the Baylor Medical Center, one of Al's largest accounts. Several Baylor staff members called for Al but couldn't reach him, and the issue went unaddressed for an unacceptable length of time. As a result, shortly thereafter the hospital purchased $250,000 of competitors' equipment. Al realized he had dropped the ball, so to speak, and that his fate was cast. Shortly thereafter he resigned without a fight.

John Rosenthal was more of a challenge. He was an old running buddy of Mark Tyler and thought that relationship made him bulletproof. His continual backstabbing and passive resistance tested Sonny's patience. Finally, even Tyler grew tired of putting up with John's lackluster results and playboy shenanigans and green-lighted his departure. When Sonny offered him the option of resigning or getting fired, John submitted his four-word written reply, "I resign effective immediately."

Dick Waltz continued his downward spiral of staying up all night worrying about his lack of sales results. Fueled by strong, dark coffee that he drank by the vat and more than occasionally boosted with a shot of bourbon, he worried rather than worked. Dick eventually jumped without being pushed. He was 57 years old and divorced three times when he married Helen. He thought he had finally found true love until he came home early from a sales road trip and found her in bed with another woman. Soon after, Helen left to explore her femininity, and Dick completely fell apart. His sales nose-dived to record depths that even he could not justify. Dick resigned and less than a year later died from a massive heart attack.

Sonny expanded the territories of his four new stars and hired one more winner. Ralph DeMata was a tall blond hard-charger from Sugarland, Texas, southwest of Houston. His boyish good looks coupled with a casual but effective sales style made him an instant success in Bob Felton's old territory. None of Bob's customers missed him. The only remaining sales rep problem Sonny had was Joe Holloway.

Sonny analyzed the Houston Service Center operation and found it to be a total disaster. The Japanese had established the branch when they first entered the U.S. market and staffed it with a strange array of individuals with seemingly no concern for ability. Besides ineffective management, lackluster customer service and slipshod technical support, the office was in an old industrial park north of Houston. Traffic in the city was bedlam on a good day, which made the branch office more than an hour away from Intercontinental Airport. Sonny soon concluded that the new office should be moved nearer the airport: the Dallas-Fort Worth International Airport.

Omniplex had a huge new repair facility in San Jose, California. The company used an exchange system for endoscope repairs to get medical equipment back into service as quickly as possible. Sonny found that by using commercial carriers that delivered direct from San Jose to Dallas, the turn-around time on repairs to his region could be reduced by two to three days. In the medical device industry, a couple of days was a lifetime.

Sonny made an impassioned plea to Opperman and Tyler to allow him to move the branch office from Houston to Dallas. He had located an attractive facility for lease in a duty-free zone near the Dallas-Forth Worth airport that would upgrade Omniplex's image and provide for expedited direct shipments from Japan. He could hire a new support team in Dallas and train them to be sensitive to customers. Opperman saw the advantages, but Tyler was against the plan for unspecified reasons. Sonny later learned that he had a favorite clerk in the Houston branch. When he was in town, Tyler met her after hours at his hotel to work on "improving her performance."

* * *

The Farmington Hills house finally sold after being on the market for almost a year. The Grahams had a desirable property but were still lucky not to take a loss. Sonny had been commuting to Houston while Joan took care of Wren and kept the house clean for the occasional real estate showing. They were happy to unload the property but sad not to make any money off the sale. Closing on the Farmington Hills house happened about the same time Sonny finally got clearance to move the branch to Dallas.

With a move to Houston no longer in the cards, Sonny and Joan began looking for property in the Dallas-Fort Worth area. It seemed that everything began moving at warp speed. He had to lease an office, complete the build-out, and hire and train the branch staff, all while managing his new sales team and looking for a new home. It was a crazy time.

Sonny and Joan found out she was pregnant again just before she accompanied him to Dallas for their first house-hunting expedition. They arrived in Dallas on the afternoon of August 2, 1985, with hotel reservations at a Marriott within walking distance of the north end of one of the airport's runways. About an hour after they had checked in, Delta Flight 191, a regularly scheduled domestic flight from Fort Lauderdale, Florida, attempted to land in a light rain.

The Lockheed jet with 152 passengers and 11 crew members on board crashed onto the highway several thousand feet short of the runway after flying through a stormy microburst. The plane skidded across the highway, crushing a car and instantly killing the driver, before smashing into a pair of four-million-gallon water tanks on airport property and exploding. One hundred thirty-six souls on board were lost in the worst accident ever to occur at Dallas-Fort Worth International Airport. The horrible event occurred within walking distance of Sonny and Joan's hotel room and was a sobering welcome to Texas for the Grahams.

* * *

Sonny and Joan bought a house being built in northern Tarrant County, west of the airport in an area speckled with horse ranches, and settled into a new life among the real cowboys and the cowboy pretenders. They paid $280,000 for the 3,800-square-foot two-story home and funded the extensive landscaping and large swimming pool and spa out-of-pocket. In January 1986, their son, Logan Graham, was born at Harris Hospital in Fort Worth. Wren, more than four years old, and the little towhead Logan completely occupied Joan's life while Sonny traveled the mid-South prodding his team to record achievements. In less than thirty months Sonny had completely revamped the Southwest sales region and taken it from last place to first in the regional standings within the Medical Products Division. The following year Sonny was named Manager of the Year at Omniplex and presented with a large mahogany plaque. The simple, elegant gold etching read:

OMNIPLEX WORLDWIDE CORPORATION U.S.
MEDICAL PRODUCTS DIVISION

1990

SAWYER "SONNY" GRAHAM
Manager of the Year

Awarded in recognition of superior achievement, outstanding contributions and distinguished service to both company and customers

* * *

As he left the '80s behind, both Sonny's personal life with Joan and the kids and his career were fabulous. He had operations at the branch office under control, his newly redesigned sales team was breaking revenue records, and his career was on the corporate fast track. But the balloon of Sonny's perfect world was about to pop because he had yet to deal with Joe Holloway.

When Sonny assumed leadership of the Southwest Region, he already knew that Joe was a problem. Joe's performance had deteriorated to a pathetic level. Though at one point he had been Salesman of the Year, Holloway had come to rank among the sales force bottom feeders. Jericho was aware of mounting customer complaints but was reluctant to take action. The Japanese at the top of Omniplex's corporate ladder seemed clueless to the problem, not wanting to lose face by admitting their top salesman had gone bad.

Saving face is an important attribute in Japanese culture; to lose face means one's self-worth is diminished. As a result, it is considered bad form to be brutally honest during business relationships. Telling someone what you really think might cause the other party to lose face. Additionally, to allow everyone in a business negotiation to save face, decisions are often made by team consensus so no one person is to blame for a poor result. To Sonny's mind, this was carried to the extreme by Omniplex's unwritten policy that no one should be fired. The company's Japanese senior management felt that if it became necessary for an employee to be terminated, then the manager must have failed to coach and encourage the worker properly. In that case, the failure was the manager's, not the employee's, and everyone in the management chain would lose face. As a result, the Japanese generally put up road blocks whenever the Americans wanted to fire a problem employee.

Tyler, who had become senior vice president of the Medical Products Division, didn't want to put his reputation on the line and risk losing face by pressing the Holloway issue with the Japanese. And because Tyler wouldn't risk being blamed for Joe's demise, Sonny was left to deal with Joe as best he could.

Sonny's business instincts told him that Joe was irretrievably damaged and could not be saved. To placate the Japanese and Tyler, he first tried to help Joe by working with him, but Joe was defiant and hostile. When no performance improvement was seen, Sonny tightened the oversight and made Joe more accountable for his time, but the complaints kept mounting. As a last resort, Sonny markedly decreased the size of Joe's territory, turning many of the VIP accounts over to Jay Draper.

Sonny knew Joe had to go, and soon, but he also knew that Jericho would have to be backed into a corner before they would deal with him. In the meantime, they were perfectly content to allow Joe to be Sonny's problem. Sonny began a meticulous process of recording every complaint, logging all the lost sales and documenting each act of insubordination.

It didn't take long before he had a damning dossier on Joe, and though Joe's pathetic sales numbers spoke for themselves, the report was so thorough and authenticated that even the most timid

Japanese would have to admit that Joe was causing critical damage to the business.

However, rather than approving termination, Tyler insisted that Joe be given another chance and put him on probation for six months. Sonny was to personally meet with Joe to deliver the news and outline the terms of the reprieve. By this time, Joe had become so unpredictable and hostile that Sonny, recalling rumors that Joe was always armed, had considerable foreboding about the meeting.

Sonny shuddered when he remembered the time he went to New Orleans to bail Joe out of a problem with an important account. Joe was so high when they met at the airport that Sonny refused to ride in Joe's car. Sonny had decided to go to the hospital alone, so he had rented a car and told Joe to go home. Sonny had watched as Joe's car crept across the parking lot and pulled in front of a toll booth with a red light clearly marking the lane closed. Joe had sat in front of the gate blocking the exit until Sonny finally got out of the rental car and pounded on his car window, telling him to move to a different lane so he could leave the parking lot. Sonny had paid the parking fee for Joe and then watched his car drive off at about fifteen miles an hour.

Sonny also thought back to the time he had received a call from Joe's long-time friend, Mary Hilton, the Head Operating Room Nurse at Our Lady of the Lake Hospital in Baton Rouge, Louisiana. Mary had reluctantly complained about Joe's service but then added, "I really was very disappointed that Joe has let his personal appearance deteriorate. He was in the hospital for the in-service of our new equipment and evidently had been eating sugar donuts before the meeting because he had sugar all over his nose and mouth." Sonny had known that Mary knew that the substance on Joe's face wasn't sugar. She just couldn't bring herself to rat Joe out on a drug charge, but she very clearly had wanted Sonny to know there was a serious problem. This proved to be the straw that broke the camel's back. Sonny finally convinced Jericho that something had to be done with Joe, and Tyler had rubber-stamped the disciplinary plan.

With much trepidation Sonny called Joe to set up the probation meeting. He had decided to neutralize the weapons issue by sending Joe a prepaid round-trip American Airlines ticket allowing only an hour and a half in Dallas. He would meet Joe at the gate and then usher him to the American Airlines Admirals Club inside security, where he would usher Joe to the VIP lounge and give him the bad news about his probation in a private meeting room. In that way he could be assured that Joe was not armed, as he would have had to clear a metal detector in New Orleans before boarding the plane and would not have a chance to leave the airport before Sonny picked him up inside the security zone at the arrival gate.

The meeting went as Sonny expected. Joe had been high and couldn't make heads or tails out of what he was being told. After summarizing the situation several times, Sonny put Joe back on the plane for New Orleans with a set of documents outlining the terms of his probation, which clearly stated that if the conditions were not met, Joe could be fired. Six months later, nothing had changed; in fact, things were much worse. But Tyler still would not fire Joe and mandated one last gambit to keep from doing so.

Tyler had gone to Omniplex President Sidney Korman behind Opperman's back and gotten approval to pay for an expensive inpatient program at a swanky Southern California rehab facility. It was a good plan until Joe refused to go. Tyler then flew a doctor friend of Joe's from Little Rock to New Orleans to try to talk Joe into agreeing to the rehab. That plan also failed. Finally, with no cards left to play, Mark Tyler reluctantly signed off on Joe's termination.

Sonny met with Joe one last time in New Orleans at an airport hotel and gave him a letter that spelled out why he was being fired. Omniplex agreed to give Joe one-month's salary and six month's commission as severance pay, plus continuing his health care benefits for six months. Joe was so whacked during the meeting he could barely talk, and it took Sonny several attempts to get him to understand he had been fired. When the light finally went on to what was happening, Holloway slurred, "Doesn't my past performance buy me anything?" With a slight smile Sonny softly said, "Joe, it bought you the past two years." All Joe could manage to say in response was, "This rotten company owes me." As Joe staggered out the door, Sonny watched from the hotel room window as he slowly searched for his car. As the new Mercury lumbered out of the parking lot, Sonny said to himself, "I hope I never see that guy again."

A MOST DETERMINED LUNATIC

ELEVEN

Something was up. Kelly Upton called on behalf of Mark Tyler and told Sonny to get to New York. He was to meet Mike and Mark for dinner at Smith & Wollensky Steak House at 49th Street and 3rd Avenue in Midtown Manhattan. The restaurant was a New York institution and super expensive. Opperman and Tyler never hesitated to spend Omniplex's money on fancy dinners, but their guests were usually VIP physicians, C-level management from partner companies or important Japanese executives from the Tokyo office. Kelly told Sonny that after the dinner he should plan on spending the next day at the corporate office. Kelly of course knew more than she would tell Sonny so he pressed her for details. "Come on, Kelly. What's this all about? I know you have some idea," he said. "Why would the M boys decide to wine and dine me? Something big must be going on." In her most sincerely placating voice, Kelly breathlessly whispered, "You know, I have absolutely no clue, Hot Shot. No idea at all." Sonny chuckled to himself, and so did Kelly.

Opperman and Tyler were already on their second drink when Sonny arrived at the restaurant and took his seat. After another round of alcohol and a massive steak dinner, Opperman called the business meeting to order. He wanted to start a new North American product group within the Medical Products Division to capitalize on the growing demand for endoscopes in family practice. Omniplex had some lower-cost gastrointestinal endoscopy equipment that was reaching the end of its product life that Opperman and Tyler thought could be re-positioned for cost-conscious family-practice doctors. In a moment of divine inspiration, they had named the new operation the Family Practice Products Group. They wanted Sonny to implement the concept from the ground up, and he would be its new director.

Sonny wanted the job. He felt he had been born for this opportunity, but before he accepted he required some concessions, and this time he was not negotiating with Tyler. Sonny stated his demands straight out to Opperman as take it or leave it. "I want Jay Draper for my wingman," he said. Mike agreed.

"I want to develop a team of younger reps and hire both men and women," he added. This would be a real departure from the current Omniplex all-male profile. It meant bucking the prevalent chauvinistic influence of the Japanese that had kept the company's sales staff an exclusive boy's club for almost twenty years. Again, Opperman nodded agreement.

"To do this right I'll need a team of field-tested managers and funding to develop a month-long training school to indoctrinate the newbies with the proper selling tools," he said. "I will demand the managers keep them on a tight leash. I want to promote six or seven experienced field reps from the existing endoscope sales force for my senior management staff." Again, Mike agreed.

Sonny understood the new position was a corporate job based in New York, but he did not want to uproot Joan, Wren and Logan. The unstated reality was that he did not want to live on Long Island with Opperman and Tyler as neighbors, where they would be looking over his shoulder constantly. Sonny said he wanted to stay in Dallas and run the group out of the Dallas branch office. He reasoned he could use some of the staff he had originally trained for support of his old endoscope region, which would allow him to get the new group up to speed quicker. Without objection Mike agreed. Then like a good trial lawyer who had the witness on the stand answering his series of questions in the affirmative, Sonny made a bold move. "I want to report directly to you, Mike." Opperman smiled and agreed. Mark Tyler silently fumed.

* * *

Jay Draper moved his family from Metairie, Louisiana, to Dallas to help Sonny with the new project. After months of preparation, the Family Practice Products Group officially launched in the fall of 1990. Sonny had been commuting in and out of New York for several months while developing the group's strategic business plan. Jay held down the fort in Dallas and began recruiting sales managers from the existing endoscope division. Sonny would come in to close the deal, and he quickly grabbed two super sharp guys for his management team. It was not a hard sell because most of the field sales reps would rather have worked for Sonny than Tyler anyway.

Sonny wasn't surprised that it didn't take too long before Tyler convinced Opperman that if left to his own devices, Sonny would stock his management pool with the cream of the crop of the Medical Products Division's sales pros. Tyler didn't want that to happen. He knew that if Sonny's ragtag band of mavericks excelled, outshining the older well-established sales force, he too would be personally diminished. Tyler was most certainly not going to let that happen.

Tyler, who would never forgive Sonny for slipping out from under him on the manpower chart, saddled him with a greenhorn marketing manager who was headquartered in Jericho. The arrangement was cumbersome at best because the rest of the family-practice group would be in Dallas. Carl Salinez was a talkative busybody who knew almost nothing about endoscopy, and very little about business in general, and would be of marginal help to Sonny. Of course, Tyler knew this. To contain Sonny, Tyler's new strategy was to deny him valuable resources whenever possible. By keeping the Family Practice Products Group's marketing support in Jericho, Tyler could keep tabs on whatever Sonny was up to because Sonny would have to communicate with Salinez, who would also be communicating with Kelly Upton.

Sonny and Jay Draper's four-week sales training class was built around principles that Sonny had mastered at Johnson & Johnson. Small groups of new hires would be brought into Dallas for four weeks of intense training. Sonny wanted to instill a sense of team spirit in the new group, so everyone would stay at the same hotel and train, eat and unwind together. Classes would meet from 8 a.m. to 5 p.m. each weekday, and the students would have the weekend off but stay in Dallas. On the middle weekend everyone could fly home to rest and relax but then would return for the final two weeks of the most intense training. On the weekends that the class remained in Dallas, Sonny arranged for a variety of team-building events, everything from bowling to Texas rodeos.

Sonny hired a headhunter and began the national hiring campaign. The first wave of recruits would be divided into four classes of eight hires each. Training would be under the direct supervision of Draper, and the sales managers would provide the close-in tutoring. Classes would consist of product presentations, videotapes of procedures, hands-on use of products, videotaped mock sales calls and a field trip to Baylor Medical Center to observe procedures first-hand. There would be written tests and a comprehensive final exam. Losers would be weeded out during the second and third weeks of testing. After the grueling training course, the remaining keepers who survived the boot camp would be turned loose on physicians across the country.

* * *

After he was fired, Joe started spending more time with Lucas Westwright than with his family. The two Red X'ers had established semi-permanent residency at a survivalist hangout in New Orleans' Ninth Ward called The Cage, so named because the dive's main attraction was a large steel cage in the center of the bar room. Every night, pro wrestler wannabes lined up to take their turn in the cage while drunks in the bar cheered the gladiators on and voted on the best performer. Winners got $25. Losers got pummeled.

The Cage was a perfect location for conducting high-level Red X business. It was dark, illuminated only by the glow of neon beer signs on the walls and the spotlights that glared down on the canvas on the cage floor. The décor was Early Depression, and the bartender had the personality of a wounded grizzly bear. There was a powerful aroma of stale beer, body odor and mold. The ambiance of The Cage was such that any sane person would pause before eating or drinking anything served there.

Joe conducted a lot of business at The Cage. No doctors were stopping by to purchase medical equipment, but there was a lively market for contraband, with hushed hustles taking place in every corner. Joe supplied cocaine, munitions and customized weapons to a variety of unsavory characters. Business was good, but he was always short of cash because he was shooting his profits up his nose. His cocaine habit had escalated to a dangerous level after his departure from Omniplex, and he was wasted most of the time and didn't bother looking for a legitimate job.

Joe's relationship with his family was collapsing at an accelerating rate in proportion to his increased use of cocaine. Just for good measure, on occasion Joe would snort a little PCP to heighten his paranoia. His brother had disowned him some time back, and his wife was now completely traumatized by him. He would spend the day at The Cage or in the swamp with his Red X friends drinking to the edge of unconsciousness. When he did sporadically arrive home it would be to continue drinking and torment Melissa. She knew not to say anything about the drinking but bristled at his open consumption of drugs in the house, where Kimberly might see him getting high, or worse, try it herself. To pacify Melissa, Joe had started dissolving his cocaine in a quart of vodka and putting the mixture in a plastic water bottle. He spent most of his lucid hours in the basement bunker boring out rifle barrels, cutting down gun stocks and modifying semi-automatic weapons so they could fire on full automatic.

When Joe came up for air, home life was an adventure into the Twilight Zone. He would be unresponsive and brooding one minute and then become amorous the next, often at inappropriate times. Melissa never knew how to react and was terrified to say much of anything. If she spoke at the wrong time and said something Joe didn't like, she would earn a swift whack to the head.

Melissa couldn't count on Joe for anything: not a pay check, not loving affection, not help raising their daughter, not even showing up at home for dinner. If he actually did commit to be somewhere he would arrive just in time to be two hours late. Melissa wanted to leave but tried to survive in place for the sake of her daughter, who was a senior in high school. When Kimberly was safe at the University of Texas she would bolt, but until then, she would keep her head down and her mouth shut.

Joe's older brother Ronald had started distancing himself from Joe some years before. By the time Joe lost his job with Omniplex, they spoke only infrequently and rarely saw each other. Ronald had a profitable legal practice specializing in real estate law in Florida and didn't need Joe or one of his scary pals showing up at his office begging for money. Before Joe was fired, Opperman had called Ronald to ask whether he would fly to New Orleans at Omniplex's expense to try to talk to his brother into rehab. Ronald turned him down cold and said he wanted nothing to do with Joe.

Their mother was a different story. Vonda was showing preliminary signs of Alzheimer's disease. She would leave the oven on after heating leftovers, report her car stolen when it was parked at the mall and forget to pay monthly bills. Ronald was gradually assuming control of her life and supplementing her savings with a monthly stipend deposited directly into her bank account. In the throes of early dementia, Vonda's children reverted to their youth in her mind. Ronald became Ronny, the high school standout, and Joe emerged as Little Joey, the unappreciated and always broke soldier.

One day Ronald opened the mail and reviewed Vonda's bank statement. He was furious to find that she had been writing checks to Joe, as he was giving money to her and she was giving it to Joe. He had tried to explain that Joe once had made more than $300,000 a year and that if he needed money it was his own fault for blowing the opportunity of a lifetime. Vonda couldn't grasp that the money she gave to Joe went right up her little boy's nose. Ronald totaled the damage and found that Vonda had given Joe more than $10,000 in a little more than 30 days.

Ronald took Vonda's checkbook, car keys and credit cards. She wasn't happy and let him know it. What she did not let Ronald know was that she had another checking account at a different bank. If Little Joey needed money to supplement his military pay, then she would take care of him.

Joe opened a notecard from Vonda one day and read, "I'm sending you $1,500 to hold you over until payday. I hope the Army isn't being mean to you,

Joey. I really hope you can come visit me soon in Oklahoma." But Vonda lived in Tampa, near Ronald. Joe tossed the card into the waste basket and pocketed the check.

A MOST DETERMINED LUNATIC

TWELVE

For several months, strange things had been randomly occurring at 704 Saddlebrook Drive in Colleyville, Texas. It was all small potatoes, nothing for Sonny and Joan to get overly worried about. First, someone shot paint balls at their mailbox. Six weeks later someone repeatedly vandalized the outdoor Christmas decorations. Sonny would replace the broken lights and smashed lawn ornaments only to find them damaged again the next week. He concluded it was probably the work of local wayward youth with too much time on their hands.

After the Grahams had gone to bed one night, a car drove through their front yard and tore up the grass. It was probably joy-riding high school kids out for a night of sophomoric pranks. When it happened the second time, Sonny and Joan figured it was more likely those damn punk kids who lived a few blocks away, the ones who were always racing mommy's new Audi through the neighborhood.

Next, the front of the house was egged. When Sonny stepped out the front door to pick up the morning newspaper one day, he found a runny, slimy substance dripping from the windows, porch overhang, shutters and two-story white columns across the front of the house. Cleaning that mess up was going to take a lot of work, so a frustrated Sonny finally called the Colleyville Police Department. About twenty minutes later, while Sonny was trying to hose the sticky mess off his house, a patrol car turned into the circular driveway. Officer Kyle O'Brian took a vandalism report and told Sonny he had seen a few eggings, most of which had occurred several months ago right before the football game between the two rival Colleyville high schools. But none had been as extensive as what he saw at the Grahams.

Then the annoying phone calls started. A couple times a week the phone would ring but when answered, there was no one on the line. At first it didn't seem unusual to Joan. They got tons of telemarketing misdials, and debt collectors kept calling for Rose Spencer, who apparently had their number before the Grahams. As time went on the calls turned creepy. A caller would ask whether Sonny was home. When Joan asked who was calling, the line would go dead. After a couple weeks someone started calling for Sonny saying he was an old Army buddy. Next, a caller introduced himself as Dr. Johnson, calling to discuss endoscopes. Joan finally realized that the same person was placing all the calls.

When Joan told Sonny about the calls his jaw tightened. A little voice from the back of his mind had been nagging him for weeks, and he told Joan he thought he knew the caller and that it was the same person who had been vandalizing their home. He had been worried about Joe Holloway since he assumed control of the Southwest sales region.

* * *

The day had been uneventful until Sonny got the call from Jimmy Shipman. Jimmy was still working for the Omniplex Medical Equipment Group in Memphis, but his territory had been expanded. He had inherited the Arkansas portion of Joe Holloway's old territory when Jay Draper moved with Sonny to the Family Practice Products Group. Jimmy stayed in touch with Sonny, calling occasionally to get the latest inside story on what senior management was up to in Jericho and swap war stories with Sonny about the "good ol' days." Jimmy and his wife, Brenda, were good friends of the Grahams. Sonny had stayed at the Shipmans' new home in Cordova, just east of Memphis, and the two couples always joined up at Omniplex award events and incentive trips. However, this day Jimmy was not calling to chat. He had disturbing news for Sonny.

Joe Holloway was spiraling out of control. His drinking was excessive several times over, and his drug use had escalated to a life-threatening level. Home life was now almost nonexistent as he was spending most of his time with Lucas. The two Brothers of the Red X were working together to sell modified rifles and other miscellaneous munitions to survivalists and to score cocaine for themselves. The partnership was working reasonably well until one night Lucas passed out in the front seat of his car while stopped at a red light. He was still lounging behind the steering wheel when a patrol car rolled up behind him. Unfortunately for Lucas, the DUI was the least of his worries: The car was stolen, and the guns in the trunk weren't registered to him, or anyone else for that matter. Lucas got ten years on the gun charge and five more for the stolen car. A previous felony theft conviction made him ineligible for parole until he had served at least two-thirds of his sentence, so Joe would have to find a new running buddy. Lucas was going to be a guest of the State of Louisiana for years to come.

Whenever Joe was at home in Destrehan he was in a nasty mood. He pushed Melissa around and on occasion worked her over. Melissa had lost all love for him and wanted to scream whenever he came near her. Because Joe was not bringing home a paycheck, to keep food on the table Melissa took a job as the bookkeeper at her brother's small automotive repair business. Unfortunately, she didn't make enough to keep her financial ship from sinking. The bank was done threatening foreclosure and filed court papers to take the house. While she was at work a loan company repossessed her car. Her brother put down a deposit and made the monthly payments on a used car so Melissa could get to work, but he did that on the condition that she divorce Joe immediately.

By this time, Kimberly had started her freshman year at the University of Texas in Austin, so Melissa packed the few clothes in Kimberly's closet and the personal effects she left behind and put them into a rented storage locker. She emptied her own closet into a couple of old travel bags and took them to her brother's house. She didn't bother to tell Joe she was leaving.

* * *

The property was engulfed in flames when the East St. Charles Volunteer Fire Department turned onto Villere Street. St. Charles Parish sheriffs' deputies were already on the scene and had used their squad cars to block both ends of the street. With flashlight beams bouncing in the dark as they ran, deputies were going door-to-door evacuating the neighborhood. A burly officer ran up to the firefighters who had arrived to fight the blaze and yelled for them to pull their equipment out of harm's way because of the danger of exploding munitions. As the orange flames licked up into the black sky, loud booms reverberated through the night air, accompanied by the steady popping of exploding ammunition. It took several hours before the impressive fireworks display subsided. When the pyrotechnics had stopped, there was nothing left of the house but the basement and the fortified rebar sticking out of the foundation where the doors and windows had been.

The next morning as the fire department started picking through the charred remains of the property now owned by the First Louisiana Mortgage Trust Company, they soon discovered a sub-basement crammed with partially melted metal ammunition cases, rifle parts and gun-making equipment. They didn't need to bring in the arson squad; they simply started at the curb, where an empty ten-gallon gas can

130

sat in the street, and followed the burnt path through the front yard to the smoldering heap of debris that had been Joe Holloway's home.

* * *

Jimmy Shipman's phone call caused the hair on the back of Sonny's neck to stand up. There was urgency in his voice that Sonny had never heard before. Jimmy wanted to alert Sonny that his wife had just discovered a slurred message on their home answering machine from Joe, who had called to thank Jimmy for being a friend and to let him know that he had torched his house and was setting out to settle old scores. Jimmy said he didn't know what to make of the call but thought Sonny should be on guard. He would contact Mark Tyler and let him know about the call. Jimmy ended the conversation advising, "Sonny, I have a really bad feeling about this thing. You know this guy is a certifiable nut case, so be careful. Watch your back."

Sonny told Joan about the conversation, breezing through the most disturbing details. He told her to be vigilant and make sure she knew where the kids where at all times. Next he called Jay Draper to notify him. "Just a heads up," he told Jay. "Nothing to be too worried about." Then he called Tyler.

131

Jimmy had already checked in with Tyler by the time Sonny called Jericho. Tyler was bemused by the situation and gave Sonny a quick wave off that he was sure nothing would come of any threats. Sonny reminded him of Joe's military training, survivalist tendencies and affinity for firearms. Tyler reassured Sonny he would talk to Mike Opperman and get back to him. Later that day, Tyler did briefly discuss the situation with Opperman, and they came to the conclusion that Joe was, as Jimmy had said, certifiably nuts but that in their assessment he was not a real threat to Omniplex.

Tyler never called Sonny back, but he and Opperman went upstairs to run the issue by Sidney Korman. Regardless of what they felt should be done, both Opperman and Tyler knew that the president of Omniplex would do whatever he wanted on his own schedule.

Opperman summoned Gill Blankenship, head of security at Omniplex's corporate headquarters, to his office. During the brief meeting Opperman gave Blankenship an overview of the situation. Blankenship was a decent guy who tried hard but was not a world-class security expert. He had been a New York City policeman before he retired and was hired to patrol the halls at Omniplex. Through the years, his title had grown with his tenure, but his expertise had not. He advised Opperman to notify all the remote facilities and said he would be on the lookout for Joe should he visit the corporate office.

A memo was sent out from Jericho to all Omniplex facilities in the U.S. alerting company employees that they should call the police if Joe was seen on the grounds of any of the company's properties. The notice said Joe was a disgruntled former employee who might be armed and dangerous. A small black-and-white photo of Joe in a suit taken at one of the company's award banquets accompanied the memo and was posted at the reception desk in the lobby of each building's main entrance. Sonny had the memo reproduced in large type with the photo blown up to an 8x11, and he personally posted the notices at a dozen locations throughout the Dallas branch office.

Omniplex Dallas had recently moved from the original 5,000-square-foot branch in the Freeport Tech Center industrial park across State Highway 114 from the Dallas-Fort Worth International Airport. The Dallas market had exploded for Omniplex as Sonny had predicted, and the local branch became a regional operations center, quickly outgrowing the old rented facility. To accommodate the growth of the business, the company leased an attractive tract of land about five minutes farther east and had the Trammel Crow Company of Dallas build a new 90,000-square-foot regional branch office, repair center, training facility, show room and warehouse. The upscale property was on a tree-lined boulevard just minutes from the clubhouse at the snooty Hackberry Creek Country Club, where the Dallas Cowboys' star quarterback, Troy Aikman, and several prominent oil and gas executives were members.

Sonny had been on the team that had coordinated the development of the facility with Trammel Crow and had carved out a large corner office in a private alcove for himself. The building opened shortly after Joe had made his phone call to Jimmy Shipman, so Sonny elected to give up his window-lined executive office to a field manager from the Microscope Division. The office had a soothing view of a small grove of flowering trees and was the prized location of the building. Instead, Sonny took a small office along the outside wall that had a view of the guest parking lot. From his new viewpoint he could see anyone entering the front of the building. Unlike the spacious corner office that was at the dead end of a short hallway, the smaller office opened into the large customer service bullpen that offered two separate pathways out of the building. If Joe came gunning for him, the escape routes would be far more important than the executive view of a grove of trees.

Sonny downplayed the strategy to Joan but he started varying the times he left the house and the routes he took to work. He didn't park in his reserved parking space near the building's front door but instead parked in the back and entered through the loading dock. The suspicious calls had stopped, but Sonny surmised that it didn't hurt to be vigilant. Maybe Tyler was right and there was nothing to worry about after all. But maybe Tyler was wrong.

A MOST DETERMINED LUNATIC

THIRTEEN

I t was an exceptionally warm day for the first week of April in Colleyville, Texas. Tropical weather was sweeping up from Mexico and bathing Northern Texas with temperatures in the high 80s. The pear trees lining Saddlebrook Drive were blossoming prematurely, and green shoots could be seen sneaking into the wintered brown Bermuda grass. Sonny left work early and headed home. He coached his son Logan's youth soccer team, and the Jaguars had a practice scheduled at the new Colleyville Soccer Complex just off Pleasant Run Road.

Logan was only five years old, but he had already been playing soccer for two years. He had started his soccer career at the YMCA in Hurst playing co-ed "ant ball," a game that was supposed to be soccer but instead always deteriorated into a mob of tiny players bunched in a tight pack kicking randomly at the ball. Logan was tall for his age, and really coordinated. He had a natural instinct for the game and had the advantage of being coached by someone who had actually played soccer, since his old man had played a little in college. Most of the dads coaching Pee Wee soccer in Colleyville knew nothing about the sport because football was king in the Lone Star State. Logan already comprehended the flow of the game and would run to where the ball was heading rather than follow the ant pack. He was going to be a good soccer player.

Six months of ant ball had been enough. Sonny moved Logan into the Under Six league run by the Colleyville Parks and Recreation Department. Because league players in this bracket could be nearly seven years old, Logan would be playing with kids almost two years older. Sonny was confident Logan could hold his own, and in fact, Logan was the best player on the team.

Sonny quickly changed out of his suit and laced up his soccer boots. On his way out the door he told Joan that practice would be over in an hour so he and Logan would be home for dinner by 6:30 at the latest. He grabbed the team kit full of balls and orange traffic cones from the garage and Logan from the back yard. The two *futbol*-ers piled into Sonny's new graphite black 300E Mercedes Benz and headed for the soccer fields.

* * *

Engine off, the Mercury Grand Marquis slowly rolled down the steep grade of Mockingbird Lane and silently coasted to a stop at the T intersection with Saddlebrook Drive. The driver in the front seat was alone in the car, and he was fixated on the property in front of him. He was on a mission.

Katherine Osborne looked out the front window of her home on Mockingbird Lane and spied the brown Mercury that she had seen cruising the neighborhood before. The driver was slumped in the front seat. Something didn't seem right, and she reported the suspicious car to the Colleyville Police Department, and then she called her neighbor, Joan Graham.

Joan didn't know Katherine Osborne well, but they had talked several times about their gardens and flowering trees so it was not a surprise for Katherine to call. But what Katherine told her took Joan's breath away. Katherine informed her that a car was parked across the street, that the driver seemed to be staring at the Grahams' house and that she had just called the police. Joan thanked Katherine, and when she rushed to the parlor to look out the window, she looked straight at Joe Holloway, who was parked less than 100 feet from her front door.

Joan panicked. Wren would be arriving on the bus from school soon, and they would be alone in the house while a crazy man sat at their doorstep. Joan had no way to reach Sonny because he was out on the soccer field with Logan, so she called a friend whose husband also coached soccer and would be at the Pleasant Run fields. Joan's hands were trembling as she hurriedly dialed the phone number of her close friend, Phyllis Duncan, who immediately volunteered to go alert Sonny and take Logan home with her. Joan would wait for Wren and hope that either the police would arrive or Sonny would get home before Joe tried anything.

Sonny was on the field putting his neophyte soccer players through some basic drills when Phyllis came running up from the parking lot out of breath. He saw her coming and thought it odd for Phyllis to be in such a hurry, but as she neared, Sonny could see the concern on her face and knew something was wrong. All Phyllis said was, "Go home! Joe's at your house." As Phyllis collected Logan, Sonny sprinted to the Mercedes and slammed it into gear. The Colleyville soccer complex was only fifteen minutes from home, but Sonny pulled into the driveway in less than ten.

* * *

Colleyville police officers Darrel Ward and Randy Ortiz yanked Joe out of his car at gunpoint after a slow-speed chase down Saddlebrook Drive. Joe had rolled away from Ward at three miles an hour and refused to stop until Ortiz used his patrol car to push Joe's Mercury to the curb. The two officers put Joe on the ground, pulled his hands behind his back and cuffed him. Joe didn't appreciate the treatment and told the officers so in no uncertain terms, but fortunately for Joe his speech was so slurred that neither policeman understood a word he said.

Crime in Colleyville wasn't exactly running rampant, so the police department's modest headquarters were somewhat underwhelming. The Colleyville Police Department shared a 12,000-square-foot building with the Colleyville Volunteer Fire Department. On one side of the cement-block building the fire department garaged a well-used pumper truck and an EMS van. On the other side, Chief Drake Steel mustered his urban troopers, most of whom had migrated to Colleyville's sedate but well-paid force from police departments in larger surrounding cities.

The Colleyville jail cells consisted of two plain-walled 8-foot-by-8-foot rooms with steel doors in the back of the headquarters building. The doors had steel bars that covered a small window and a slot with a slide used to pass food into the cells. Bolted to the wall directly across from the door and in full view of the window was a platform covered with a thin mattress. At the end of the bed was a steel combination sink and toilet affixed to the floor.

Joe wasn't cooperating with officers Ward and Ortiz as they forced him from the patrol car into the police station. Once inside he struggled with the booking agent, who called for support to get him searched, stripped to his underwear and into a dark-blue jumpsuit. For the mug shot, Ortiz pinned Holloway to the wall, and Ward held him by the chin to keep his head straight. It took almost an hour to get Joe into his cell.

Once inside the cell, Joe began kicking the door. Ignoring multiple orders to stop, Joe continued ranting until three officers entered the small room and tried to take him to the floor. Suddenly, the overweight inmate became a superman, refusing to give an inch to the officers. Fueled by drugs, Joe positioned himself in the corner of the small room and repeatedly fought off the officers. He held his ground until two more officers joined the fray and the group overpowered him, forcing Joe to the ground. Once he was pinned, the group manhandled him into a straightjacket and left him struggling on the floor.

* * *

Officers Ward and Ortiz began a thorough search of the brown Mercury that had been towed to the impound lot behind police headquarters. They had already recovered a water bottle from the front seat that looked as if it had something dissolved in the liquid. They also found a small knife from the driver's side door pocket. But it was not until they popped open the car's trunk that they saw they had stumbled onto something out of the ordinary.

It would take them several hours to inventory the trunk's contents. The list included:

Guns:
Colt Government Issue Model Mark IV .45-Caliber Revolver, Serial #91143G70
Colt Combat Commander .45-Caliber Revolver, Serial #70SC37516
Charter Arms Bulldog .44-Caliber Revolver, Serial #566390
Charter Arms AR-7 Explorer .22-Caliber Rifle modified to full automatic, Serial #A120895
Sturm-Ruger Mini 14 .223-Caliber Rifle modified to full automatic, Serial #18215467
Sturm-Ruger Mini 14 AC-556 .223-Caliber Rifle full automatic, Serial #19936222

Scopes:
Redfield Revolution Reticle Riflescope 3.3-8.5 magnification, Serial #APZ37810
Leupold VX-R 1.25 4x20 Zombie Rifle Scope, Serial #Z1200306

Knives:
Colt M7 Fighting Knife with M8A1 Scabbard
Conetta Mark 2 Fighting Knife with sheath
Buck Knives Model 110 Folding Hunting Knife
AlMar SERE Special Forces Knife
Buffalo P172 Folding Knife

Ammo:
(250 rounds) Federal Ammunition 5.56x45m NATO
    rounds, full metal jacket
(200 rounds) Winchester 5.56x45mm 55 gr. full metal
    jacket
(550 rounds) Federal .22-Caliber copper-plated

Goggles:
ITT Optical SU49/PAS5 Night Vision Goggles, Serial
    #US49P2773082

Gas mask:
US Military M17 Gas Mask with leather case

Wigs:
Woman's blond 15-inch length wig
Woman's gray 8-inch length wig

Clothes:
Women's size 14 knee-length floral dress
Women's size 14 knee-length navy blue dress
Women's size 14 black parka
Women's size 10 black flats

Money:
$4,000 in U.S. currency
$8,000 in Danish kroner
$8,000 in Deutsche marks

Maps:
New Orleans, Louisiana
New Orleans Rivergate Convention Center
Tarrant County, Texas
Jackson, Mississippi
Nassau County, New York
Denmark
Germany

I.D.:
Passport: Joseph Vincent Holloway (USA)
Passport: Vernon J. Von Andersson (Danish)
Passport: Gunther Haussman Gröbel (German)
Driver's License: Joseph Vincent Holloway (Louisiana)

Journal:
Hard-cover hand-written journal in black

* * *

Chief Steel peered at Joe Holloway through the small barred window in the holding cell at police headquarters. Three hours after having been forced into a straightjacket, Joe was still prone on the floor fighting unseen demons. The chief shook his head. In all his years of police work, this out-of-control display was one of the most severe he had witnessed. Steel wanted this lunatic out of his jail as soon as possible, but he knew Holloway was too wired for transport to the Tarrant County Jail.

Steel was a by-the-book twenty-year veteran of the Dallas Police Department, and after his retirement, he served as the assistant chief of police in Arlington. Chief Steel had been the head law enforcement officer in Colleyville for three years when Holloway came to visit. Steel carried himself like a military man and resembled a mature Cary Grant, his snow-white hair in striking contrast to his navy-blue uniform. At 6 feet 3 inches and a trim 190 pounds, Steel looked as though he had just stepped off a 1950s Hollywood movie set.

Steel returned to his office and called his friend of thirty years, Tag Thompson, the sheriff of Tarrant County. Steel told Thompson that he had a "problem child" locked up in Colleyville that he really needed to unload on Fort Worth. Sheriff Thompson didn't think twice before he shot back his three-word reply: "Bring 'em on!"

Steel kept Holloway twelve more hours before he felt comfortable having him transported to 350 West Belknap Street in Fort Worth, where the three-story Tarrant County Inmate Processing Center is located. Colleyville rarely had a hardened criminal in custody. Lots of petty thefts, pill heads, wife abusers and drunk drivers had taken up brief residence in their small cells, but Joe was special. Steel knew this case file was going to land squarely on the desk of Tarrant County District Attorney Chet McKinney. Steel took the extra precaution of sending a trailing patrol car as backup to the black-and-white SUV chauffeuring Holloway to Fort Worth.

A MOST DETERMINED LUNATIC

FOURTEEN

His custom-built house reduced to cinders and his freedom at least temporarily gone, Joe Holloway's new home was the Tarrant County Jail in Fort Worth. The jail had four facilities spread throughout the county, but the largest of these was the Greenbay Confinement Unit, the county's primary place to lock up criminals.

Because Greenbay housed inmates ranging from low-level offenders to those being held for violent crimes such as robbery, rape and murder, it was accredited as a maximum-security state prison, with a security level equal to any maximum-security state prison in the nation. The thousand correctional officers who worked there had all been certified by the Texas Commission on Law Enforcement to use force to deal with the most violent inmates.

Tarrant County's sheriff, Randall "Tag" Thompson, was responsible for the operation of the county's correctional system. Two-thirds of his annual budget went to operate the county's four jails housing more than 4,500 inmates, and most of that was spent running Greenbay, which he controlled with a strong hand.

Sheriff Thompson got his start with the Dallas Police Department as a standout at its academy. He earned the nickname "Tag" as a rookie patrol officer working a bad neighborhood on the south side of Dallas. Thirty years and fifty pounds ago, he ran down a small-time felon after a protracted foot race, and upon tackling the luckless criminal told him, "Tag. You're it!" His nickname was born on the spot. During a spotless street career, he was commended several times for his volunteerism and excelling in his job.

Tag Thompson's Stetson-wearing officers had a solid reputation as a no-nonsense bunch who could take care of business. Although a large percentage of Tarrant County knew the force only as the sheriff's horseback posse that rode in the Fort Worth Stock Show and Rodeo Grand Entry parade, Tag's boys routinely dealt with the most difficult offenders the county had to offer.

Tag Thompson's office was on the seventh floor of the Tarrant County Plaza Building in downtown Fort Worth. He didn't routinely visit the Tarrant County Correction Intake Center, where all the county's inmates arrived to be prepared for housing in one of the four jails. But Tag was on site to greet the prisoner his friend Chief Steel had sent to him. Holloway arrived on schedule in a drug-induced stupor wearing a straightjacket, leg irons and a plastic helmet because he kept banging his head on the wall of his cell in the Colleyville holding tank.

* * *

After Sonny raced home from the soccer fields, he first reassured Joan that they were safe, then he called Omniplex. He informed Michael Opperman that Holloway had just been arrested across the street from his house and that he was confident Holloway was there to kill him. Opperman brought Mark Tyler in on the call, and after a brief conversation it was agreed that Omniplex would engage a local attorney to determine Holloway's incarceration status.

Two hours later Johnny Jay Lovett, a flamboyant Fort Worth-based criminal attorney, called for Sonny. Omniplex had retained him to use his considerable connections to keep abreast of the Holloway case.

151

Sonny had seen Lovett on television a couple of times always expounding on the perceived wrongs done to his clients by the Texas judicial system. Lovett, a short, sandy-haired native of Fort Worth who was never seen in public without his Stetson cowboy hat, introduced himself in an unmistakable Texas drawl.

Lovett had made some inquiries and called in some favors because he was only too happy to assist a wealthy corporation that would pay twice his standard rate for some quick action. Talking to a confidential contact in the sheriff's office, he learned that Holloway was being transported from Colleyville and would be held in the Greenbay unit until he was arraigned. Lovett also volunteered that acting on his recommendation, Opperman had hired an executive protection company to evaluate the risk to Omniplex employees and that someone from Texas Corporate Protection would be calling Sonny within the hour. Lovett said he would follow up with Jericho and then closed with an impassioned pitch to represent Sonny should he need to take legal action against anyone or anything, ever.

About 45 minutes after hanging up with Lovett, there was a knock at the Grahams' front door, and Sonny looked out to see a well-dressed business executive flanked by two men in uniforms standing on the front porch. John Ragetty introduced himself as the chief executive officer of Texas Corporate

Protection and, as Lovett had said, announced that he had been hired by Omniplex to protect the Grahams.

Ragetty had started his law enforcement career as a patrol officer with the police department in Arlington, the third major component of the Dallas-Fort Worth Metroplex, with a population of slightly less than 300,000 in 1990. Ragetty was a good-looking, smooth-talking, energetic guy with a quick mind and big aspirations. He soon grew tired of the daily grind of writing speeding tickets and directing traffic at accident scenes. He worked nights so he used his days to enroll in the business school at the University of Texas-Arlington and graduated with a bachelor of science degree in business management.

With a freshly printed college diploma and still in his early 30s, Ragetty quit the police force and started a company that provided event security. He landed a big contract with the historic Dallas Cotton Bowl, home to the Texas-Oklahoma football game, to provide security guards for their major events. He used the job as a springboard to secure contacts with the rich and famous in the Dallas-Fort Worth area. Within two years, Ragetty had talked his way into a lucrative contract with a Fort Worth multi-millionaire protecting the oilman's business, home and family. Soon his company had an established list of elite clients that included sports figures, local TV personalities, a prominent politician and high-end business executives. As he knocked on the Grahams' leaded-glass front door, business was profitable and Ragetty was on the top of his game.

Seated in the parlor of the Grahams' home, Ragetty relayed a grim story to Sonny and Joan that made them both more than a little nervous. Since being contacted by Lovett on behalf of Omniplex, he had shifted his staff into high gear making phone calls and working with the resource firm his company used to run background checks. In short order, Ragetty had received preliminary information on Sonny, Holloway, Omniplex and the Medical Equipment Division's top two executives from his staff. He personally spoke to Chief Steel at the Colleyville Police Department and Detective Cary Mortan, who was investigating the Holloway case for the Colleyville police.

Ragetty detailed the problem, which was much worse than Sonny had imagined. As he explained what he had learned to Sonny and Joan, it became clear to Sonny why Opperman had Omniplex cough up the money to hire executive protection before he had even asked for help.

First, there was the list of contraband confiscated from Holloway's car, which Ragetty said had the lethal firepower of a small army. Next, there was the journal. Ragetty skipped much of the details, but there was a list of names in the book that police believed was a hit list. Looking Sonny squarely in the eyes, Ragetty flatly said, "Your name is on the list." Finally, there were the disguises, the maps and the foreign currency. To Ragetty it was clear that Holloway intended to pursue the names on the list, then skip the country after he satisfied his lust for revenge.

Then Ragetty dropped the big bomb. After talking with the various law enforcement agencies involved in the case, he believed that Holloway would not be deterred in his efforts to exact retribution. If he should be cut loose from Greenbay unexpectedly on a technicality or a clever move by a hired legal gun, Holloway would more than likely come right back to the Grahams' house. The protection company had thus made arrangements for the Graham family to spend a few days away from their home.

Ragetty told Sonny that his family would be under the constant protection of his experienced personnel, who were highly trained in personal protection. All were former policemen, sheriff's deputies or Texas Rangers, and they would be on guard round the clock. His company had a hotel suite in Fort Worth where the family would be safe while Ragetty's boys guarded the house. When Joan asked when they would go to the hotel, Ragetty said, "Right now!"

Joan quickly scooped up some clothes, a few toys and a couple of books for Logan and Wren, then packed a small bag for herself. Sonny threw clothes into a duffle and grabbed his briefcase. Before they really understood what was happening, the whole family was in a nondescript dark-green van, followed by an equally nondescript dark-blue sedan, heading for the Worthington Hotel in downtown Fort Worth.

Dubbed "The Star of Texas," the Worthington was Fort Worth's original AAA Four-Diamond luxury hotel. In the heart of historic Sundance Square, the hotel was a majestic landmark surrounded by cobblestone streets, gaslights and Fort Worth police on horseback. Texas Corporate Protection had reserved a group of rooms on the eighth floor of the hotel. Coming off the elevator, the Grahams, Ragetty and two of his best men turned left and walked twenty feet to a short hallway perpendicular to the main hallway.

Three doors opened onto the hallway, which came to a dead end just past the last door. The door to the first room was open, and Sonny could see a bank of television monitors on a credenza. Wires ran across the floor from the monitors and down the hall to where multiple video cameras were installed, giving the occupants of the first room full view of anything that moved in the hallway. Sonny also noted several shotguns lying on the bed.

Near the end of the hallway there were two rooms, one on either side of the hall. On the left, double doors opened to a large suite with a small kitchen, a large cherry dining table with six high-back leather chairs, and a living area with two upholstered loveseats in front of a media cabinet housing a television, stereo system and a videotape recorder. The outside wall was lined with large windows that looked down on Sundance Square next to the hotel eight floors below. Hard candy filled the glass bowls on the end tables; a selection of leather-bound books had been carefully placed on the shelves next to the TV, and a variety of magazines lay on the massive glass-topped coffee table in front of the sofas. Fresh-cut flowers were arranged in a glass vase on a writing desk in one corner of the largest hotel room Sonny and Joan had ever seen. Directly across the hall behind a single door, the family found a sleeping room with a king-size bed, a walk-in closet and a spacious marble bathroom. Along the wall bracketed by two richly upholstered Queen Anne armchairs, a TV sat on a massive wooden credenza.

Logan and Wren ran back and forth between the rooms giggling with delight. The fact that they were excited about staying in such a magnificent hotel was a major bonus. They thought it was an adventure that would be great fun, a family camp-out with room service.

But Sonny and Joan were still in shock.

Ragetty gave the Grahams a couple hours to settle into their upscale accommodations before he walked Sonny down the hall to the security room while Joan and the kids explored their new living quarters.

Once inside, he introduced Sonny to two officers of Texas Corporate Protection stationed in its hotel room command center. Danny Peters was a veteran policeman who was now a shift supervisor for Ragetty's company. Michael "Big Mike" Knight was a hulk of a man who had been a Tarrant County sheriff for many years. Both were seasoned professionals skilled at executive protection. They were now dedicated to protecting the Grahams.

* * *

The daily booking report at the Tarrant County Correction Center told the story in black and white:

Holloway was now also known as inmate no. 0386215, and he was processed at the correction center before his transfer to Greenbay under the personal supervision of Sheriff Thompson. At the reception center Holloway was photographed, finger-printed and strip-searched. He was issued a gray prison jumpsuit with the large black letters TC JAIL on the back. After a brief physical exam, Holloway was transported across town to John Peter Smith Hospital for a visit with a psychologist.

After thirty minutes talking with Holloway, Dr. Da Hong Shang, a graduate of Guangdong Medical University in China, determined that Holloway was crazy but that he was not legally insane and sent him back to Tag Thompson's supervision.

* * *

Ragetty spoke to Sonny with an urgent tone, dispensing with any pleasantries, and got right to the point: "Joe Holloway is an extremely scary guy, and he possesses weaponry to kill someone from a mile away. Sonny, you will never see him coming. From what I've learned about this guy in a short amount of time, I would say he's not above doing anything because he appears to be a complete loony tune."

Although the case against Holloway seemed ridiculously simple, a slam-dunk, Ragetty cautioned Sonny on the realities of the judicial system. Holloway was a first-time offender with a solid work history. The drugs found dissolved in vodka were only a trace amount and not enough for a serious drug charge. If the water bottle had been full rather than empty, police could have charged Holloway with something meaningful. The weapons in the trunk were registered to Holloway, and, although some had been modified, he did not have a gun on himself when he was arrested. It was not illegal to have wigs, money, clothing and maps in the trunk of your car, so no charges would come from that. The fleeing and resisting-arrest charges would probably get tossed because the chase never got faster than five miles an hour. Then Ragetty gave Sonny the really bad news. A sharp lawyer could probably spring Holloway without breaking a sweat, and if that happened he would be right back on the Grahams' doorstep. There was, however, some good news. Ragetty had a plan.

Ragetty, who detailed this plan with Sonny in private to shelter Joan, told Sonny that Holloway wouldn't give up. The journal found in the Mercury contained phases such as "check out after mission" and "go down fighting" and "settle all old scores." Holloway was dedicated to going out in a blaze of glory. Ragetty then told Sonny about the map of the outside of the Graham home that was found in the journal in Holloway's car. Ragetty didn't hold anything back. "It's a crude but detailed drawing that could have only been made by someone who has been on your property, who has walked around the house and taken notes," he said. "Holloway has been stalking you for some time and is getting close to taking action."

The journal was a rambling record of his demented thinking that outlined a vague plan of revenge against a number of people, including Sonny; Lloyd Holt, who was one of Sonny's sales reps with no known connection to Holloway other than that he took over part of Holloway's old sales territory after Holloway was fired; Melissa Holloway's divorce attorney, Grover Wilcox; and two unknown Brothers of the Red X identified only as "Ted and Jepson." The last entry on the list was Omniplex Worldwide.

Given a copy of the entire journal by Chief Steel, Ragetty had taken it to Mary J. O'Donnell, a private-practice psychologist on retainer to Texas Corporate Protection, and asked her to evaluate Holloway's threat level. Ragetty gave Sonny a copy of Dr. O'Donnell's written report, which read:

* * *

March 13, 1991

Mr. John Ragetty - CONFIDENTIAL
Chief Executive Officer
Texas Corporate Protection
100 East 15th Street
Fort Worth, Texas 76102

Dear Mr. Ragetty:
Following is my impression regarding the journal you provided to me. Please keep in

mind that this report should not be construed as a formal diagnosis, since I have not personally interviewed the subject who wrote the notes, but are my impressions of the type of person who might have written them.

This individual is clearly extremely emotionally disturbed, and his difficulties began when he was a young child. He appears to have failed to develop a basic trust in others, perhaps because his first experiences were with people who failed to understand his needs and to respond empathically.

He perceived early in life that he would have to protect himself from others and would have to compete for the fulfillment of his basic needs. He also saw himself as different or as not fitting in with the people in his life, and he has remained somewhat aloof or isolated since. He arms himself for the competition of life, as he sees it, by remembering in great detail his exchanges with others and by keeping a running credit/debit sheet in his mind. During trying times, he recalls who might owe him something and calls in his markers, or at least fantasizes about doing so.

His self-styled tendency to be a "workaholic" may also be an effort to arm himself for the competition, and he apparently did so with a vengeance. He probably uses drugs: amphetamines, cocaine, and such would be expected as drugs of choice. As a suspicious guarded person he probably turned to speed because it helped him remain hyper-vigilant. Unfortunately, speed appears to exacerbate paranoid potential. Alcohol may have been used abusively to medicate the effects of stimulants, to allow periods of rest. He would have achieved his career goals at any cost and having done so would feel his employer owed him and therefore would be honor-bound to take care of him during difficult times.

It appears that his emotional problems began to totally overwhelm him, his marriage failed, and eventually the loss of his job and the ending of his marriage saw him severely overcompensate.

He is a poor judge of how others perceive him. He has deep-seated doubts about his own achievement but cherishes awards, plaques, gifts and kudos he has received as proof of his worthiness.

From the journal, it appears that the subject perceives himself to be at the end of the line. He is desperately attempting to balance the books, right wrongs done to him and "settle scores and check out." He is methodical in his planning. He lives in a magical world where he could rid himself of all interlopers and restore "the natural order." He feels a need to explain his planned suicide by leaving a note that convicts his father of emotional abuse and, secondarily, his mother of making poor choices.

He appears to be extremely dangerous as he feels he has nothing to lose. He may be reckless despite his careful planning. When he gets close to his target, it would not be wise for an untrained person to try to restrain him. He may very well be somewhat daunted by his recent arrest and may take some time to reassemble his wits and reorganize his plan. If he does not move immediately, it appears he will continue to pursue his subject at all cost and will eventually close in on the target.

Finally, and of high importance, if he is being apprehended, he is very likely to pull a last-ditch stunt such as opening fire on those who are approaching him, then on himself. He must be approached with the highest degree of caution.

Regards,
Mary J. O'Donnell, Ed.D
Psychologist

Ragetty saved the worst for last, and what Sonny heard next made him sick to his stomach. Ragetty frowned as he said, "In the normal course of developing background on the case, I sent an agent to both Logan and Wren's schools. A teacher at the First Methodist Church's Tiny Tot Day Care Center has identified a picture of Joe Holloway as someone she had seen in the school. A review of the school's video surveillance tapes confirms Holloway's brown Mercury in the parking lot and picked up Joe as he strolled casually down the main hallway. He could be planning to target your kids, either to hurt them to hurt you or to grab them to draw you to him. Either way, the kids are in extreme danger."

Ragetty paused a minute to let Sonny digest what he had just said and then divulged the rest of the sad story. Using Joe's journal, numerous police reports, the videotapes from the pre-school, jailhouse snitch intelligence and the analysis of the psychologist, Texas Corporate Protection had developed a probability scenario. It concluded that Holloway did in fact plan to kidnap one or both of the Graham children and hold them as bait to draw Sonny out into the open. Once Sonny came for the kids, Holloway planned to ambush him using one of the sniper rifles that had been found in the car.

Finally, Ragetty arrived at the end game. While the family was camping at the Worthington Hotel, three of Texas Corporate Protection's best men were hiding in the Grahams' house in the event that Holloway was released from Greenbay. Guns were positioned around the property, and shooting lanes had been established. The plan was simple: If Holloway showed up at the Grahams' home, he would be allowed, even encouraged, to enter the house. Once he entered the house, he would not leave alive.

A MOST DETERMINED LUNATIC

FIFTEEN

It seemed that Chet McKinney had been district attorney of Tarrant County forever. He had been a fixture on local television and at galas and civic events for twenty years but was rarely seen in the courtroom. With a staff of 300, including more than 150 lawyers, the District Attorney's Office was the largest law firm in Tarrant County, disposing of more than 35,000 cases a year. McKinney had a reputation as a solid administrator and a consummate dealmaker when it served the judicial process, and foremost, his political career. Over the years, his propensity for opting out of tough cases with plea deals got him labeled "No Trial McKinney."

McKinney reviewed the file on Joseph Vincent Holloway and did not like what he read. Mr.

Holloway was a dangerous man. There was plenty of evidence to show that he was a menace to society, but the case could be problematic, and there were lots of potential pitfalls for the prosecution. A major international corporation was involved, which could mean high-profile lawyers, nosy press and, eventually, public awareness. McKinney expended a considerable amount of energy trying to avoid getting involved in this type of matter. However, he was far too clever to get caught without a plan. He picked up the phone and returned the call of Johnny Jay Lovett.

* * *

Sidney Korman summoned Michael Opperman and Mark Tyler to his office on the top floor of the Omniplex headquarters in Jericho. Unlike the dog-eared offices of the peons on the lower floors, Korman's command center was opulent. His personal assistant, Dorothy Stillman, sat guard outside heavy wooden double doors that led into a small anteroom with paneled walls covered in expensive artwork. A second set of doors opened to the main office, which was large enough that a small army could have held maneuvers in the room. Natural wood floors covered with expensive Persian rugs and subdued drop lighting set the tone for the decor. The office was in the corner of the building with two solid glass walls offering a panoramic view of the woods along the parkway behind the office complex. Across from the entry, a single door opened to a private bathroom that featured a tiled shower and small cedar-lined sauna. Sidney's massive antique cherry Queen Anne desk was fronted by three leather wing chairs. In the middle of the room two upholstered sofas sat facing each other separated by a large hand-carved cherry coffee table, and polished-brass lamps perched on end tables next to the sofas. The room was designed to impress, but Korman seldom allowed anyone other than Dorothy Stillman to enter his private sanctum.

Korman was born on Long Island and lived his entire life within a few miles of his boyhood home. The dutiful son of a doting mother, Sidney was a small, effeminate intellect who was bullied at school and ignored by his father at home. He had few friends and spent most of his free time practicing piano because his mother believed he would become a famous concert soloist. Sidney dreamed of playing first base for the Chicago Cubs, but he had no skill, and besides, Ernie Banks had permanently secured that job.

Korman graduated from high school with honors, then attended Hofstra University, where he earned a bachelor of science degree in business. While at Hofstra he met and married Rachel Wasserstein, the only girl he had ever dated. The newlyweds settled down in a little bungalow less than three miles from

Korman's mother's house. His uncle ran a surgical supply company in Queens and created a sales job for him. He did well enough to attract the interest of a competitor and left his uncle's company for more money and a shot at management.

When Omniplex Worldwide entered the U.S. market with their new line of high-powered and optically superior surgical microscopes, Korman was one of the first field sales agents the company hired. He established himself as an aggressive sales presence, and within a couple years he was running the fledgling but extremely profitable microscope division. His take-no-prisoners style offended many of his associates, but his sales results endeared him to his Japanese bosses.

Fourteen years into his career at Omniplex, he was running the most profitable product group but seeking greater status. Korman maneuvered behind the scenes trolling for the president's job when the senior Japanese executive was recalled to Tokyo. Much to the disappointment of many of his colleagues who feared his dictatorial nature, his campaign was successful. Sidney Korman was named the first American-born president of Omniplex Worldwide U.S.

Korman was agitated and demanded an update on the Holloway situation. "This damn thing has already cost the company $20,000, and John Ragetty's meter is running 24/7," he fumed. Opperman patiently informed him, "Holloway is in jail, and the Grahams are in hiding. It's a very bad situation."

He said the executive protection company felt Holloway would eventually get out of jail and probably would renew his pursuit. Korman asked whether either of his executives had discussed the company's legal exposure with Aaron Silverstein, the corporation's in-house attorney. Opperman said yes: "I met with Silverstein, and the news is not good on several fronts."

Opperman then detailed the scope of the problem: "First, if Holloway injures or kills anyone connected to the company, including a family member of an employee, Omniplex will surely get sued since the crisis developed from a work-related situation. Second, Sonny Graham is apparently Holloway's primary target, but that cannot be assured. In his diminished mental state Joe might decide to go after another company employee, or worse, a group of Omniplex workers."

Attempting to curry Korman's favor, Tyler interjected that the chances that Holloway would actually get to anyone at Omniplex were minimal and that he thought the cost of protection was excessive. Opperman glared at Tyler, continuing as if he hadn't spoken. "Third, Gastroenterology Week is in New Orleans this year. That's Joe's hometown."

Gastroenterology Week, a medical convention attended by 8,000 gastroenterology physicians, 3,500 specialty nurses and 2,000 technical exhibitors, would be held in sixty days at the Rivergate Convention Center in New Orleans. The convention was the Medical Equipment Division's largest technical exhibit and sales meeting of the year, and the company would have nearly a hundred personnel on site for the convention. Opperman looked straight at Tyler when he said, "If Holloway somehow gets into the convention hall and shoots up our exhibit, the money that is being spent to protect Sonny Graham will be small potatoes compared to Omniplex's liability after a massacre." This was not what Korman wanted to hear, so he gave Opperman a look that said, "You had better come up with some better news fast."

Korman was indignant. "What am I supposed to do?" he said. "Omniplex can't afford to provide private protection for every attendee at the convention." Opperman said he understood Korman's point but continued, "If the company does not take adequate precautions, the outcome could be financially devastating for not just our operations here in the U.S. but for Omniplex Worldwide." Tyler's silence spoke volumes about his level of support of Opperman.

Undeterred, Opperman continued, "I hired a local attorney to assist with this matter. His name is Johnny

Jay Lovett, and he has been in contact with the Tarrant County district attorney. Together they hatched a plan to put Holloway on ice with limited fanfare. Lovett will call Holloway's brother, Ronald, and speak to him lawyer-to-lawyer. Johnny Jay will try to get Ronald to sign commitment papers for Joe and file them with the court. Once done, the district attorney in Fort Worth will get the presiding judge to commit Holloway to the North Texas State Mental Hospital in Vernon for an indeterminate period. The hospital provides maximum-security forensic psychiatric services." Opperman closed saying, "Given the advanced degree of Holloway's mental state, it is more than likely that the hospital in Vernon will be Joe's home for the rest of his life." Korman exhaled an audible sigh of relief.

* * *

After returning from his psychological evaluation at John Peter Smith Hospital, inmate no. 0386215 settled into the leisurely life of a convict at Greenbay. Roused from his bunk bed at 6 a.m., he would slip into a less-than-fashionable jumpsuit and a pair of plastic slippers. Breakfast of a granola bar, a piece of mystery meat, a greenish orange and a plastic bottle of apple juice arrived from room service through the slot in the door a half-hour later. Breakfast was followed at 7 a.m. by a stimulating hour of sitting in "the pit," a large, open room where all the steel furniture was bolted to the floor. While in the pit, inmates could watch television, play cards, talk among themselves or privately sulk in a corner. From 8 a.m. to 11:30 a.m., inmates labored in their assigned work areas such as food preparation, janitorial services and grounds maintenance. Not taking into consideration his previous careers as a combat medic, milkman and high-tech medical products salesman, Holloway was assigned to work in the prison laundry.

A nutritious but tasteless lunch consisting of a bologna sandwich, a piece of fruit, a slice of cheese and a cup of Jell-O was served at noon. At 1 p.m. everyone reported back to work and busied themselves doing as little as possible until 4 p.m. The remainder of the afternoon provided for one hour of solitude staring at cracks in the cell ceiling from the rock-hard bed with the only diversion being thirty minutes of inactivity in the recreation yard. At 5:30 p.m., give or take twenty minutes, a tasty gourmet meal such as packaged spaghetti with chicken meatballs, frozen mixed vegetables, a slightly stale slice of white bread and a cup of instant chocolate pudding for dessert was served in the formal dining room. The dining room was a large windowless room with long tables and hard benches secured to the floor. The walls, at one time painted solid white, were now stained a light gray. Guards standing in little alcoves off the main room watched the diners enjoy their *haute cuisine* through bulletproof windows. After the evening meal, the pit was reopened for the inmates to enjoy unlimited amounts of boredom.

Ragetty's mole in Greenbay was Stewart Edwards, a longtime Tarrant County sheriff who served as a guard at the jail during the week and moonlighted with Texas Corporate Protection on the weekends. Edwards had been told to keep an eye on Holloway and relay back anything of interest to Ragetty's company. It wasn't long before Edwards called in a report. Holloway wasn't eating. He was overweight so on the surface it seemed he could be trying to shape up before his court appearance, or it might be that he just didn't like the food in Greenbay. But on closer look, Edwards discovered Holloway was trading food for a treasured prison currency: cigarettes. This was curious, as Holloway didn't smoke. Ragetty feared he knew why Holloway was hoarding smokes.

* * *

Holloway soon discovered that he had friends on the inside, a couple survivalists who were also in Greenbay. Nelson Smith and Lester Newcastle were both from Texas but at one time had done business with the Brothers of the Red X in Louisiana. Smith was serving the last two months of his sentence for threatening a peace officer, and Newcastle had thirty days left on a domestic abuse charge. Holloway shared a lot in common with his two new best friends. They were all crazy for guns, and they were all crazy. Holloway spent most of his considerable free time with Smith and Newcastle. He supplied them with cigarettes and impressed them with tales of his exploits with the Red X band of brothers.

* * *

After about ten days encamped at the Worthington Hotel in downtown Fort Worth, the Graham family was starting to show signs of cabin fever. Television had been watched, cards had been played, and room service meals had been devoured. Joan was helping Wren put together a puzzle from the hotel gift shop while Sonny and Logan were playing soccer on a makeshift field in the bedroom across the hall. The boys used as goals two chairs placed in front of the king-size beds and played with a soft, fuzzy soccer ball. The game on the 6-foot-by-18-foot floral carpeted field was spirited and sometimes loud, but there were no other guests on the floor to complain. Occasionally a lamp would take a direct hit, but no serious damage was done. Sometimes Wren would join Logan's team for a two-on-one match against Dad. When they tired of soccer, Sonny and Logan switched to armadillo football, passing around a plush stuffed animal that had previously been caged in the gift store.

* * *

Opperman, the lead dog of the Omniplex endoscope division, had placed a lot of faith in the strategy concocted by District Attorney McKinney. However, their plan was dead on arrival once Opperman called Ronald Holloway. The older Holloway sibling flatly refused to commit his brother to an institution and said their mother would have nothing to do with the scheme either. Opperman tried to reason with Ronald and when that failed, tried to shame him into action. But Ron stood firm. Joe was on his own.

When Opperman called attorney Lovett to shoot down the mental commitment balloon, he received even more discouraging news. Lovett told him McKinney didn't want the Holloway case cluttering up his docket. If Holloway's family wouldn't go along with confining him to a mental hospital, then he would plea bargain the case out of existence.

* * *

It was a beautiful spring day, and the flowering crabapple trees lining the cobblestone streets around the Worthington Hotel were in full bloom. Looking out the window of the suite, Joan was in a melancholy mood. She was tired of doing laundry in the sink and eating room service food. She felt trapped like an animal in a cage. The family had been cooped up in the hotel for almost two weeks while waiting on the courts to deal with Holloway. She wished she had never heard his name. She hated him for interfering with her perfect family, and she wanted him out of her life. However, she never considered the plan that Ragetty had in mind.

Danny and Big Mike were playing Nerf baseball with Wren and Logan in the hallway outside the security room when Ragetty came around the corner. The sight of two fully armed musclemen in military-style uniforms playing ball in a hotel hallway with the little kids was quite a sight. Ragetty laughed to himself as he knocked on the double doors at the end of the hall. He had stopped by to outline a change of plans to Sonny and Joan and hoped he could convince them that it was a positive development.

Ragetty sat down with them to explain that Omniplex was balking at the expense of keeping the Grahams in a luxury hotel indefinitely. Once again breaking ranks with Opperman, Tyler had sided with

Korman and supported curtailing the cost of the current security operation. After talking with his covert contacts in the District Attorney's Office, Ragetty reported that it appeared Holloway could be turned loose at any moment. He strongly believed it was not safe for the Grahams to go home.

A small tear glistened in the corner of Joan's eye as she looked away from Ragetty and stared blankly out the window. In a subdued, almost robotic voice, she asked, "Is Omniplex abandoning my family?" With the savvy anticipation of a seasoned policeman, Ragetty offered a prepared answer, most of which was true.

He explained that although the bigwigs at Omniplex were concerned about the ongoing cost, Opperman was a strong advocate for them and carried a lot of clout in the boardroom. Opperman believed Holloway's threats were real, and he was determined to protect Omniplex and his employees and would stand up to the pressure to reduce protection. Ragetty continued that given the current situation, Texas Corporate Protection had revised the budget and presented Omniplex with a new, less-expensive plan. The family should not go home because the risk was too great, and the guard's unmentioned killing zones were still in place. There remained a strong possibility that Holloway would be back at the home within days. So as an alternative to Camp Worthington,

Ragetty's new strategy relocated the family out of Fort Worth. The Grahams were on the move again, this time to about forty minutes south of Fort Worth to scenic Granbury.

* * *

Historic Granbury is the seat of Hood County. An incorporated area with a strong rural flavor and a population just a notch above 5,000, it was on Lake Granbury about thirty-five miles south of Fort Worth. Founded in 1887, the city was named after a brigadier general in the Confederate Army, Hiram B. Granberry, who wasn't particular about how he spelled his last name.

Granbury and Hood County have a rich Texas history. In 1853, **Davy Crockett's** widow, Elizabeth Patton Crockett, settled in the county. Texas provided land in Hood County to the survivors of the men who had died fighting at the Alamo during the revolution against Mexico. Elizabeth Crockett, who died in 1860, is buried in a state park just six miles from the city limits. A large statue marks her grave site, which is the smallest state park in Texas at just twelve by twenty-one feet. Crockett's descendants still live in Hood County.

Lake Granbury, a massive manmade reservoir, was created in 1969 on the southeast side of

Granbury, and was one of three lakes damming the Brazos River. The 8,300-acre lake is contained by the De Cordova Bend Dam and has more than 100 miles of shoreline. Over the years, Lake Granbury had become a popular get-away for Dallas-Fort Worth residents seeking relief from the sweltering Texas summers.

* * *

John Ragetty pulled a black Chevy van through the gate into the parking lot at the Granbury Lodge on East Pearl Street just off U.S. Highway 377. A dark-green four-door sedan followed close behind with Danny Peters at the wheel and Big Mike Knight riding shotgun, literally. The lodge was a two-level condominium complex along the banks of Lake Granbury about five minutes from the city's old town square. Ragetty had rented two attached first-floor units under a phony corporate name. The security room that Texas Corporate Protection had established next to the Grahams' suite in Fort Worth at the Worthington Hotel had been redeployed to the Granbury Lodge next door to the unit reserved for their clients.

Garrett and Patty Phillips and their two children, formerly known as the Sonny Graham family, emerged from the van under the watchful eyes of their protectors and entered the condo next to the security unit. Ragetty joined them inside the waterfront retreat.

The rental unit featured a narrow entryway opening into a large room with a wall of windows looking out at Lake Granbury. The room décor was "lake casual" done in a cowboy motif with an overstuffed leather sofa and two leather recliners. A new color TV was positioned across from the sofa in a huge rustic media cabinet, and Indian area rugs covered the hardwood floors. Behind the sofa, a six-foot-wide brass Texas Lone Star ornament adorned the wall. Sliding glass doors opened to the boat dock less than fifty feet from the unit. A dozen or so ducks strolled along the dock unaware that they were within range of enough firepower to turn all of them into less than a memory.

An unobstructed view of the water was also available from the small kitchen, separated from the living room by a countertop lined with bar stools. Next to the kitchen doorway, a staircase ascended to a large open loft bedroom overlooking the living area below. From the second level the bedroom had a spectacular panoramic view of the lake. Sonny and Joan would sleep in the loft while the children shared the pullout from the leather sofa in the living room. The first night, Wren and Logan were delighted to be sleeping in the living room where they could fall asleep watching Disney videos on the big-screen TV.

Sonny and Joan were less than delighted to find that the loft offered no privacy for the adults.

* * *

The distinctive roar of a powerboat out on the lake could be heard cruising past the condo as Sonny and Joan sat down with Ragetty to hear the latest revision to the master security plan. Logan and Wren had been sent outside with their new playmates, guards Danny and Big Mike, to explore the greenbelt between the rental unit and the shore. Joan kept an eye on the kids as they romped around the pier chasing a little brown hoppy toad. She knew the kids were well-protected but still was concerned because they had no fear. Sonny and Joan had tried to gently explain the situation to the children without terrifying them, but they were so young that it was difficult to help them understand the problem. How do you tell a 9-year-old to fear for her life or explain to a 5-year-old that a bad man might be trying to kill him?

A MOST DETERMINED LUNATIC

SIXTEEN

John Ragetty explained the several reasons why Sonny and his family had been moved to Granbury. Foremost was the need to meet the financial constraints placed on the protection company by Omniplex. The condo was far more reasonably priced than the Worthington Hotel, and it would be a bonus that at the lodge they could do laundry and have home-cooked meals. Also, the private condo was more secure than the public hotel because the gated entrance limited access to the property. Last, should Holloway get out of jail unexpectedly, he would not be looking for Garrett and Patty Phillips in Granbury. Only three people knew where the family had gone, and they were all at the lodge.

Ragetty told Sonny and Joan, "Holloway has a

court date in ten days. He has been denied bail, but the deal to commit him to a mental hospital never really got off the ground." Ragetty went on to tell them, "I suspect Joe is up to something at Greenbay. He has befriended two inmates, and they were spending a lot of time together. Joe has been hoarding cigarettes and giving them to his loser friends. Experience tells me that exchange is some type of payment. But for what I'm not sure."

Joan was concerned about Wren falling behind in school, but Ragetty was prepared. He had been in touch with Chief Steel in Colleyville, and Steel tasked Detective Mortan to go to Colleyville Elementary School, pick up Wren's textbooks and homework assignments, and deliver them to Texas Corporate Protection. Danny Peters would be the supervisor in charge of the Granbury detail, and he would deliver Wren's assignments to the lodge. In addition, Mortan had made arrangements to pick up the Grahams' mail. For the Grahams, living in a small community with a responsive police force had advantages.

Next, Ragetty went through the ground rules for the stay at the lodge. Four guards — Danny Peters, Big Mike Knight, Larry Kendrick and Ted Holtz, whom everyone called Hoppy — would work overlapping shifts. At least two guards would be in the security unit at all times when the family was in the lodge. If the family needed to get groceries, do laundry, go to a movie or whatever, the trip would need to be planned. When the family was away from the lodge, one of the officers would remain behind to make sure no one entered the condo, and at least one guard would travel with the Grahams. Should Sonny and Joan need to go in different directions, at least one armed guard would travel with each of them. None of the family members was ever to go outside without a guard with them.

Meanwhile, Sonny was becoming increasingly worried about work. He had not been in contact with Jay Draper, the Dallas branch office or the corporate office in Jericho since leaving for the Worthington Hotel almost three weeks before. His new division was in the middle of a national hiring campaign and launching a new product line, and he was missing in action. He needed to get back to work. Ragetty assured him that Jericho knew about the relocation and understood he would be unavailable for some time. That didn't make Sonny feel any better.

* * *

Holloway looked like he had been run over by a bus. After a month in Greenbay he had lost some weight but still appeared bloated. His face was pudgy, and his complexion was pasty. Large dark bags had formed under his eyes, and he sported several days of gray beard stubble. His hair, once dyed jet black, was starting to show significant amounts of gray and was badly in need of a trim.

Life in Greenbay was easy enough for Holloway once he came down from the high of alcohol, cocaine and PCP that he'd been traveling on for far too long. He fairly quickly settled into the routine of working in the laundry and plotting with his new survivalist friends. Holloway had big plans for his prison buddies, but first he needed to endear himself to them to make sure they would stick to the strategy.

After almost three weeks of daily chitchat Holloway confided to Newcastle and Smith that he needed their help to deal with his nemesis, Sonny Graham. He outlined a plan of revenge and offered them each $1,000 cash for their help. The inmates were somewhat sympathetic to his plight and, more important, desperate for cash, so both signed on without hesitation. But there was a catch.

Before Weasel Newcastle and Snuffy Smith would do his bidding, they wanted Holloway's help dealing with a problem of their own. The two had smuggled some uncooked potatoes out of the kitchen along with a large box of refined sugar. Without having the components to build a still or the expertise to run one on the off chance they actually got it built, the two budding entrepreneurs developed a business plan to market cell-made hooch to other Greenbay numbskulls and pocket a small fortune. They had yet to work out how they were going to conceal the production facilities and inventory when a fellow malcontent snitched them out to a guard. After losing their potentially lucrative revenue stream and spending ten days in solitary confinement for having contraband in their cells, Weasel and Snuffy swore an oath to punish the snitcher. So with malice on their minds they enlisted Holloway to their cause.

The snitch was a lovely fellow named Dustin Wiltson who was called Ruby Lips by his prison lovers. He wore his jumpsuit open to the waist with the pant legs and sleeves rolled up as far as possible. His shoulder-length brown hair was done up in an attractive bun that sat on the back of his head. The large hairball sprouted two short ponytails, tied with pink ribbons, which bounced wildly as he pranced through the corridors of the cellblock. Dustin, aka Ruby, was known to spontaneously break out into song and dance for no apparent reason. He had an extensive repertoire of show tunes for any occasion, no matter how inappropriate. Mediocre at best as a song-and-dance man, as a snitch, Ruby was a headliner.

Ruby had gotten under the survivalist duo's skin on more than one occasion, and getting them tossed into the cooler was the last straw. With Joe's help, Weasel and Snuffy planned to teach the little gypsy a serious lesson he wouldn't soon forget. The plan was simple: Just before the end of personal hygiene time, when the inmates leave their cell block to use the communal showers, Holloway would come on to Ruby and get him to remain behind in the shower on the pretense of having a romantic interlude. Weasel and Snuffy reasoned that Ruby wouldn't suspect anything was afoot because Holloway had no known issues with Ruby and would close the deal with the offer of $100. Snuffy would create a distraction in the hallway outside the shower to divert the guard's attention while Weasel slipped back into the shower to confront Ruby. Holloway was to hold the victim while Weasel turned him into a pin cushion with a thin piece of aluminum that once had been the identification plate on a dryer in the prison laundry. Weasel had rubbed the metal on the cement floor of his cell until it had a razor-sharp point.

The shower room in Greenbay Cellblock D was a large cinderblock room with no windows or doors. On the wall opposite the opening from the hallway, a concrete countertop held a row of ten metal sinks with a polished metal mirror above each bowl. Alcoves to the left and right each had eight leaky showerheads that jutted from the wall and shot lukewarm water at the inmates. Bolted to the floor in the center of the room were several metal benches where prisoners could leave their towels while showering. A strong smell of disinfectant permeated the room along with a heavy humidity that was present even when the showers weren't running. While not the perfect love nest, the shower room was ideal for ambushing unprotected prey.

A MOST DETERMINED LUNATIC

SEVENTEEN

Thursday was Personal Hygiene Day for Cellblock D in Greenbay. At 7:30 p.m., the cells of Ward 1 clanged opened, and twenty soiled residents stumbled into the corridor in their skivvies to be ushered as a group to the showers by three disinterested guards. Joe was fourth in line, followed by Ruby Lips a couple men behind him, with Weasel Newcastle and Snuffy Smith bringing up the rear.

Once the group arrived at the shower room they were given twenty minutes to shower and shave before the guards started hassling them to finish and get back in line for the return trip to their cells. The time limit generally was not a problem for a number of reasons. First, the lukewarm water didn't promote long, leisurely showers. Second, a significant percentage of the inmate population had little concern for regular personal hygiene experiences and thus gave the outing only cursory consideration. Third, and most important, the shower wasn't a safe place, and the longer one tarried there, the greater the personal risk.

Joe played his part well and soon after entering the shower moved close to Ruby. A negotiation was held and a deal closed with just a few words. As prisoners finished showering and filed out of the alcove, Joe and Ruby hung back, moving to the far corner away from the entrance. Just as the showering lovebirds drifted toward each other, screaming could be heard from the hallway as Snuffy began his performance. His one-act play consisted of accusing one of the other convicts of inappropriately touching him as they stood in line. The drama ended with Snuffy coldcocking the unsuspecting inmate and drawing a crowd that included the three guards. The first guard slammed Snuffy to the ground while the second pinned his arms and slapped on a pair of handcuffs. The third guard used the radio clipped to the epaulet on his uniform to call for backup. In short order, six more burly officers arrived and began manhandling the few spectators who had not responded to instructions to line up against the wall.

Those who weren't moving at an appropriate speed were shoved, and the few who didn't move at all got a hard rubber baton to the calf. Soon all but two of the inmates from Cellblock D were back in line. One of the missing would be carted away to solitary confinement. The other lay on the shower floor.

At precisely the same time the curtain was going up on the double bill of the Snuffy performance in the hallway and the Joe-and-Ruby show in the shower, Weasel was moving at lightning speed across the shower room toward Ruby. As Ruby turned toward the noise in the hall, Joe grabbed him from behind, pulling his arms backward. Within a split second Weasel was plowing into Ruby and rapidly stabbing him three times in the ribs with the sharp point of the filed metal strip. If Ruby had been deemed a dead man walking, the attack would have been to the neck with hopes of slashing open his carotid artery, causing him to bleed out in a few seconds. But the stabbing was merely payback for the foiled business plan and an unmistakable warning about the dangers of future snitching. The wounds would not be critically deep, but Ruby would be sore for weeks and need about a dozen stitches.

Weasel probably would have preferred to stab Ruby a couple more times, but during the third penetration the aluminum stiletto broke off in Ruby's side. Joe let him drop to the shower floor, and he and

Weasel eased out into the hall, where the ruckus Snuffy had created was just being brought under control by the guards. As Snuffy lay handcuffed on the corridor floor he looked up to receive a quick head nod from Weasel. The show was over, and the deed had been done. Unless Ruby really wanted to get killed, his story would be that he didn't see who stabbed him and didn't even remember exactly what happened in the shower. Weasel and Snuffy were now in Joe Holloway's debt.

* * *

A cold wind and light snow flurries were blowing around the entrance to Omniplex's corporate headquarters in Jericho as Mike Opperman pulled his dark gray BMW sedan into the parking lot. At 7:15 a.m., there were few other cars in the lot, but he recognized Mark Tyler's new metallic-midnight-blue Audi sports coupe parked near the front door. Opperman parked next to Tyler's car and hurried into the building.

Opperman was born in St. Louis Park in Hennepin County, Minnesota, a white-collar town of about 30,000 in the central part of the state. The son of a butcher, Opperman grew up in a comfortable but modest middle-class home. He attended St. Louis Park Senior High School with about 1,800 other

Orioles and made good grades. Mike played football for the "Orange and Black" for three years, and though he was not one of the super studs in the class, he had an active social life primarily because he was a nice guy.

After high school he attended St. Cloud State University, the state's second-largest public university, for two years before transferring to the University of Minnesota. With a degree in business management, Michael exited college for St. Paul with a new wife and a job with 3M Corporation's Health Care Products Group. The marriage didn't work out, but the job did. He covered the state for 3M and excelled at medical products sales. He built a comfortable life but longed for a bigger challenge with a top tier surgical products company. He got his wish when Omniplex came calling in the mid-'80s.

Opperman was in the first sales class that the Japanese hired for their new U.S. endoscope division, and he quickly distinguished himself as a sales leader. Within fours years he was running the multi-million-dollar sales division and living on Long Island. He hadn't remarried, but he did have an almost secret off-and-on relationship with his administrative assistant, Debby Towlin. Debby accepted the arrangement because she loved her boss, but he was married to the business and didn't have room in his life for another wife.

Opperman had a difficult day ahead. He had been told to prepare a cost forecast for Sidney Korman projecting how much the Joe Holloway situation would cost the company during the course of the next six months. Opperman had called a special meeting with John Ragetty to run the numbers. They toiled over the cost projections based on the most likely scenarios that Texas Corporate Protection could envision playing out in the short term. The least expensive budget was based on the possibility of Joe getting out of jail within the next couple weeks and immediately returning to the Grahams', where Ragetty's men would engage him in a short gun battle and blow Joe away. Everyone understood that this scenario would save Omniplex a lot of money. More expensive projections had Ragetty's agents tailing Holloway for months as he crisscrossed the country stalking his various targets. One very costly contingency had Texas Corporate Protection providing undercover security for the Omniplex personnel attending the upcoming Gastroenterology Week in New Orleans. There was well-founded fear that Holloway might try to make a major statement by shooting up the entire convention hall.

Ragetty felt the most costly plot line involved a combination of all the different scenarios. The final projection was staggering, well into the middle six figures. However, Opperman knew that he and

198

Ragetty had never discussed the most costly potential outcome. That would be Sonny Graham, and possibly his entire family, being killed by Holloway right after Omniplex cancelled the corporate security they had been providing. Opperman shuddered as he thought about such a storyline being picked up by NBC's "20/20" or CBS's "60 Minutes": "Omniplex Worldwide Abandons Slain Executive to Save Money." A quick calculation put the risk factor from this projection in the tens of millions of dollars.

Opperman knew he would be asked to project the company's maximum exposure, to try to more accurately pin down a cost for what he considered to be the unthinkable finale, so he had met secretly with his corporate attorney, Aaron Silverstein, to discuss the cost of being found complicit in a wrongful-death lawsuit. He didn't like what Silverstein had to tell him, and the attorney didn't sugarcoat the bad news. "Mike," he said, "if a wrongful-action lawsuit were to be filed in a state where juries don't mess around when a little guy gets trampled on by a big rich corporation, just the process of defending the case could cost the company a couple of million dollars. If the verdict went against us, and it most likely might in Texas, it could cost Omniplex upward of $50 million." Opperman closed his eyes, not wanting even to consider telling this to Sidney Korman.

Silverstein went on: "There are ways the company could mitigate the damages. Of course the best outcome would be to win the case outright. From what I know at this point I would have to say I think this is unlikely. More costly but still a good result would be to prevail on appeal. We could also get out from under this thing by offering an attractive settlement or by treating the issue as an ongoing expense and amortizing the legal cost over several years. If you want to operate under that particular plan the company could take every legal avenue available to prolong the case until it became difficult for the plaintiff to continue to pursue their legal action. The longer the case is active, the more likely something could happen to favor the company. Attorneys might leave the case; witnesses could die, or evidence could vanish. By delaying as much as possible but continually forcing a costly legal response from the plaintiffs, Omniplex could run the family out of money, eventually stripping away their financial ability to pursue the case. Then, when the timing appears right, which by the way would be when the survivors appear to be at their weakest, we could sweep in and offer a lowball settlement." Opperman cringed at the thought of resorting to such shady legal tactics.

Concluding his observations, Silverstein pointed out that any of the scenarios he presented could likely bottom line at several million dollars. He saw no way Omniplex could come out a financial winner if Holloway killed Sonny. But then Aaron offered Opperman a remedy they hadn't previously considered. "What if Omniplex agreed to relocate the Grahams out of the United States so Sonny could work with one of the company's affiliates in Europe or Asia?" he asked. "The likelihood of Holloway finding them would be minimal, and the cost of the relocation would definitely be less than what Omniplex would have to pay Texas Corporate Protection to keep Sonny alive stateside." Opperman was silent as he contemplated the proposal, and for the first time during the meeting his face looked optimistic.

Thinking about Joan and the kids, Opperman realized this wouldn't be the ideal end game for the Grahams. Moving out of the U.S., possibly for many years, and bringing up the kids in a foreign country couldn't be what the family had in mind. However, as a practical solution, maybe Silverstein had hit on something. It might be a workable solution, but he wouldn't present it to Korman, at least not yet. He knew that if Korman saw a way to reduce the payout, he would jump on the idea without thinking it through. No, Opperman would hold the relocation plan in reserve.

At 8:55 a.m., Opperman and Tyler entered Korman's world and parked at his conference table, waiting for the inquisition. Following true Korman Time, the 9 a.m. meeting began when Sidney walked into the conference room at precisely 9:24 a.m. Opperman outlined the present security situation and the various scenarios developed by John Ragetty, then handed out a multipage financial projection. The figure on the bottom of the page was not the number divined by Ragetty. Opperman had redlined that number already — cutting the original estimate by fifty percent — and he still was distressed by it. In his gut, Opperman knew Korman would choke when he heard the amount. He just hoped old Sidney wouldn't choke him.

The financial report sent Korman into an eye-popping, neck-bulging rage. "There is no way on God's green earth Omniplex is spending $10,000 to $20,000 a week into infinity to protect one measly employee from a bumbling drunk," he said. "Do you realize we are talking *at least* $50,000 a month here? I don't give a goddamn how scary Joe Holloway is, I am not throwing that kind of money down a rat hole protecting Sonny Graham, or anyone else for that matter, from some non-specific and improbable threat. From what I hear, that son-of-a-bitch Holloway is so drugged out he probably can't tell his own ass from a hole in the ground. I don't care how good that pretty preppy boy John Ragetty thinks he is, he isn't worth $20,000 a week." At the height of Korman's diatribe, Mark Tyler interrupted. He had been content to let Opperman carry the water to this point but now saw an opportunity to trump him.

Tyler spoke up to suggest a possible alternative to spending the money that Opperman was proposing. He had come up with an idea and met with Aaron Silverstein to discuss whether to relocate the Grahams to the Omniplex subsidiary in England, Keystone Medical. With one move they could save the company mega bucks and rid themselves of the Sonny Graham problem for good. Korman might have been interested, but he expressed no opinion. Opperman was dumbstruck that Tyler would try such a bold end run but said nothing.

In actuality, Kelly Upton, Tyler's assistant, had tipped him about Opperman's confidential conversation with the attorney. She had eavesdropped on the meeting by opening the phone line to the conference room and listening in on her headset. Once clued in by Upton, Tyler went to Silverstein for a briefing on the meeting under the pretense that Opperman had cleared him for the update. Armed with potential game-changing information, Tyler went into this meeting with Korman willing to sit back and see which way the wind blew. When he saw the opening, he took it, figuring the reward would outweigh any conflict with Opperman.

* * *

Ragetty had arranged for Big Mike and Danny Peters to watch the kids for a couple hours as he and Hoppy Holtz drove Sonny and Joan into Fort Worth. One of the largest gun shows in the nation was under way at the Amon Carter Exhibition Center, and Ragetty wanted his clients to arm themselves for personal protection, knowing there was no guarantee that his boys could stop Holloway. They had to be vigilant one hundred percent of the time; Holloway had to find only one opening.

The exhibition center was in the Will Rogers Memorial Center, a massive 120-acre complex on the southwest side of Fort Worth that was named for the famed American humorist. The Original Fort Worth Gun Show was a huge two-day event and one of the country's premier gatherings of firearms enthusiasts.

Ragetty explained that it was important that Sonny and Joan each have personal protection available at all times and that they felt comfortable using weapons on the chance that his agents could not reach them in a panic situation. He would guide them around the exhibit hall and be available to consult on any purchases, but the decisions would be their own.

He recommended that they look for a good shotgun and a couple revolvers as a starting point.

Walking into the exhibit hall was an overwhelming experience, especially for Joan, who had never held a firearm in her life. The airplane hangar-sized building was crammed full of tables piled high with weapons of every size, shape and color. There were handguns, rifles, shotguns, machine guns, swords, knives, bows and arrows, and ammunition. On sale were military uniforms, gas masks, chemical gear, tents, prepackaged meals, water purifying equipment and all types of camouflage gear. There were tattoo artists, hunting experts and quick-draw shooters on small stages set up around the hall entertaining mesmerized enthusiasts. It was truly a spectacle to behold.

With attendance in the tens of thousands, the people-watching opportunity at the exhibit alone was worth the price of admission. Tax accountants pressed elbows with Hells Angels, and cowboys bid against preachers. Neo-Nazi militants bartered with school teachers, while avid collectors sold to undercover agents. The amount of money changing hands was staggering, and the number of weapons being sold could have armed a Third World country. Sonny and Joan found the extravaganza mind-boggling.

After an hour and a half walking the hall, Sonny had selected a short-barreled shotgun with a pistol grip and two semi-automatic revolvers, a .40-caliber Glock 22 for himself, and a compact Glock 19 for Joan. Glocks had originally been designed and built for the Austrian military, and the handguns had become the sidearm of choice for U.S. police departments in recent years because they were durable and accurate.

Sonny also bought a Belgian-made 6.35mm Baby Browning semi-automatic pistol with a two-inch barrel, black matte finish and brown plastic grip. To holster the weapon, he bought a black nylon ankle holster with a Velcro strap. Sonny signed a purchase agreement, was given the registration papers and was handed his new weapons in a plastic bag. In less time than it takes to pick up the kids' school books, Sonny was better armed than most small-town police officers.

Two days later, Ragetty and Hoppy Holtz again escorted Sonny and Joan from Granbury to Fort Worth. This time Ragetty had made an appointment for the Grahams to meet a friend: Tony Lacasa, a former FBI agent who ran an exclusive gun club and firing range in the basement of the Bass Building on 4th Street right in the heart of Cow Town. Several notable oil and gas bigwigs, wealthy cattlemen, and current and former professional athletes belonged to the Fort Worth Executive Gun Club. Texas Corporate

Protection put all their new security agents through a rigorous gun class run by Lacasa at the range.

Ragetty was aware that Sonny had been a military policeman in the Army and knew his way around a gun, but Joan had never held a weapon of any type. Ragetty feared as much or more for her safety as he did Sonny's. Joan didn't know the depth of Holloway's planning and that she and the kids were likely primary targets. Holloway had been to the kids' schools, and he had photographs of the kids playing in the front yard and had watched Joan backing her car out of the driveway. He had a detailed drawing of the outside of the Grahams' home that could have been made only by someone who had walked around the property.

Ragetty knew there was a strong possibility Joan might have to defend herself and her children. He knew that deviants like Holloway often selected victims from the weak or unprepared. He wanted to do whatever he could to train Joan to take the appropriate action if necessary given the time and budget constraints with which he was operating. In this case the appropriate action would be the use of deadly force.

A MOST DETERMINED LUNATIC

EIGHTEEN

Joan Graham, or Patty Garrett, as she was known in Granbury, sat alone at the counter in the kitchen of the lakeside rental, not drinking the coffee cooling in her cup or looking at the magazine she was holding. Big Mike had escorted Sonny into Fort Worth for the final round of interviews of sales candidates for the first class of his new Omniplex division. Alone with her thoughts, her mind drifted a thousand miles away as she tried to recall her wonderful life before Joe Holloway. She loathed him. How could one demented lunatic undo her lovely life so completely? She had a loving husband, great kids, a beautiful home. She felt fulfilled in her role of homemaker and mother. She longed for a leisurely shopping spree at her favorite supermarket or an hour on the phone with one of her girlfriends. Tears rolled down her cheeks and dropped onto the magazine cover. She noticed that the guards had torn off the address label before they delivered the mail to the condo. All sorts of small precautions like this were taken every day so the cleaning lady or people she encountered in town wouldn't question the identity ruse. Someone might innocently say something that could be overheard by a Holloway confederate. No one knew for sure how many people he had enlisted to help him pursue the family.

Joan couldn't use her credit cards, drive herself to the cleaners, or even call her kids by their real names. Everywhere she went, a large man carrying a concealed weapon followed her. This was definitely not the plan she had mapped out in her mind when she married Sonny what seemed like an eternity ago.

Sunday was Easter. Logan and Wren would normally get up early to hunt for colored eggs hidden around the house. They would find their Easter baskets, holding hard-boiled eggs they had already colored, sitting in the hallway full of candy eggs and chocolate bunnies. After the egg hunt the family would eat a quick breakfast, then dress up for the mid-morning service at Colleyville Baptist Church. They would return home at noon, and Joan, who was an excellent cook, would prepare a gourmet meal for the family and any guests who might be in for the holiday. Graham family tradition dictated that Easter dinner include a baked sugar-cured ham, mashed potatoes with brown gravy, green bean casserole, yeast rolls and some type of special dessert. Joan missed the solitude of working alone in her kitchen.

The Grahams hadn't been to church or talked with friends since the phone call from neighbor Katherine Osborne alerting Joan to the brown Mercury stalking her house. She cried as she thought about Holloway stealing the fun and reverence of Easter from her children. Logan and Wren had been so good. They didn't complain about missing their playmates or school. They didn't even whine about not being able to go outside whenever they wanted or without a couple guards trailing along.

In fact, in a strange way the children looked at the situation as a great adventure. They had their parents' undivided attention; they were staying in an expensive condo on the lake, and they had two new playmates who wore blue uniforms and carried guns.

Danny Peters sensed that Joan was starting to break down and worry about the impact of the confinement on the kids. She had shared with him her sorrow that they had no playmates, might fall behind in school and would miss all the Easter pageantry at church. Peters felt sorry for the friendly young family caught in a tragedy not of their own making. He would try to do what he could to help.

Peters knocked on the condo door and asked Joan whether he could speak to her privately for a minute. He hoped he wasn't intruding, but he wanted to tell her about his plan. With her permission, he would like to bring his wife and three kids to Granbury for lunch on Easter. The weather report was for a sunny day with temperatures in the mid-70s, so his wife would make a picnic lunch for the two families to enjoy behind the condo at the water's edge. He had cleared the plan with John Ragetty, who had agreed to launch his sleek new speedboat at the public boat ramp on the north side of Lake Granbury and take everyone for rides. All Peters needed was Joan's blessing. Joan cried as she gave him a big, long hug.

* * *

Sonny arrived at the Harvey Suites Hotel on State Road 114 just off the north end of the Dallas-Fort Worth International Airport at 8:30 a.m. with a fully armed Big Mike Knight in tow. He had a busy day of interviews scheduled to fill the second training class for his new sales team. Jay Draper and the other managers had conducted the preliminary interviews and selected their candidates. Each was presenting to Sonny two prospects, from whom the winning recruit would be selected.

Having Big Mike sit in on the interviews might have sent most of the sales candidates fleeing from the hotel, so Sonny had him stay out of sight during interviews. At 6 feet 4 inches and a solid 248 pounds, he was formidable. Wearing an inexpensive, ill-fitting blue suit jacket over his bulletproof vest made him appear larger than his already ample size. His blond crew cut, bulging biceps and shoulder holster didn't quite fit the image of the stereotypical GQ-dressed Omniplex sales manager.

Big Mike looked more like an announcer at a professional wrestling match than a high-tech medical equipment executive. To accommodate his desire not to let Sonny out of his sight, a two-room suite had been rented for the interviews, and a closed-circuit TV system had been installed between the rooms. This would let Big Mike sit in the bedroom and watch the business being conducted in the interviewing room. Interviews were scheduled all day, and none of the candidates ever knew there was a large man with a loaded shotgun sitting just a few feet away.

* * *

Sidney Korman called yet another emergency meeting to discuss what he had come to refer to as "the Sonny Graham situation." He had tabled the idea of transferring Sonny out of the country and relocating his family because it would cost too much. However, with the New Orleans gastroenterology convention fast approaching, something had to be done. Michael Opperman had beaten back Mark Tyler's attempt to undercut him with the relocation gambit by getting the president of Omniplex Worldwide to focus on the danger Holloway presented to everyone at the company, including Korman.

Opperman laid out a worst-case scenario for Korman that had Holloway sneaking into the New Orleans Convention Center, where he had worked medical meetings dozens of times, opening fire on the Omniplex booth and killing scores of company employees and VIP doctors. Opperman said the damage done to the company's image would be worse than the hundreds of millions of dollars they would lose in lawsuits and lost business. Omniplex might never recover from such a tragedy.

Even penny-pinching Korman couldn't disagree with Opperman's assessment. Omniplex would have to take exceptional security precautions in New Orleans. He approved a plan for Texas Corporate Protection to staff the Omniplex booth with armed undercover agents during the meeting and provide special VIP protection to key corporate executives, Sidney Korman foremost among them. But to compensate for the expense in New Orleans, Korman ordered Opperman to cut Texas Corporate Protection's expenditures in Texas by half immediately and phase out the Grahams' protection altogether after the New Orleans convention.

Opperman called Ragetty and said he thought Korman had lost his mind. He didn't want the Grahams' protection to end, for both personal and professional reasons. From the business perspective he felt the company's exposure was so serious he must protect the Grahams lest they be harmed and sue the company for millions. On the personal side, he had hired Sonny and knew he had given his all for the company. He couldn't turn his back on him at such a perilous time. Opperman told Ragetty he would find a way to continue to cover the cost of a scaled-down security detail for Sonny from his division's internal operating budget, but he didn't want Korman or Tyler to know about it.

Ragetty respected Opperman for making such a decision. He had grown close to Opperman during their brief forced acquaintance and thought he was a good man doing the best he could in a bad situation that had been dropped in his lap. Ragetty liked Opperman almost as much as he distrusted and disliked Tyler. He saw Tyler as a slick opportunist who would sell his mother into slavery if the payoff were great enough. More than a few other people felt the same way.

Ragetty also liked the Grahams. He had worked with a lot of senior executives over the years, and most were a bit phony and overly self-absorbed. Sonny and Joan seemed really down-to-earth. They had terrific kids and had led a normal life until Holloway showed up in Colleyville. Ragetty pledged to Opperman that he would not stand by and let Korman abandon his clients. He would adjust his fees and eat some of the expenses to help Opperman bury the remaining cost so they could keep constant security available for the family.

* * *

On a conference call with Opperman and Ragetty, attorney Johnny Jay Lovett relayed the latest on the judicial progress of Holloway's case. In his heavy Texas drawl he reported that the attorney whom Joe's brother had procured to represent him had twice sought to free him on bail. But as Lovett proudly proclaimed in his most sincere self-serving manner, "I worked with an assistant district attorney to squash the request. As a result, Joe remains in the Greenbay unit of the Tarrant County Jail at the present time. But that's going to change, and probably sooner rather than later."

Lovett was a short man in a big cowboy hat, but when he talked he was seven feet tall. His Texas twang came through loud and clear as he informed Opperman and Ragetty, "Our illustrious, or should I say blusterous, District Attorney Chet McKinney has decided to dump the Holloway case. He's going to let him plead guilty to a first-time drug offense in exchange for dropping all the other related charges. McKinney's deal means the most severe punishment Holloway will get will be a modest fine and probation for a year or two."

Then Lovett dropped his voice for dramatic effect as he delivered the worst news. Through his stellar undercover work, he had learned that McKinney had cut a back-channel deal with Ronald Holloway. "You know, they're both attorneys and speak the same 'we can make this situation work for us' language," he said. "Both want this problem to go away quickly."

Ronald Holloway really did have no intention of interacting with his brother and really didn't want to be involved in any way, but he had pledged to McKinney that he would make every effort to get his brother into rehab and then seek ongoing psychiatric care for him upon his release. For his part, McKinney would arrange for Joe to be given deferred adjudication on the drug charge in exchange for agreeing to leave Texas and not return for two years. Lovett added a critical caveat: "Of course, the court will have no way to monitor the provisions of the agreement."

That meant that within a few days Holloway would be released from jail and kicked out of the state, but he would be free to resume his quest for revenge at his leisure. Ronald Holloway had sprung for the cost of a one-way plane ticket to Tampa for his brother, but he had skillfully not agreed to accept any responsibility for him once he left jail. Lovett closed with emphasis: "I know it doesn't make a lot of sense, but the way Mr. McKinney has crafted his plea deal, Joe Holloway will be free and clear of all current charges and have a clean criminal record in Texas if he just pays a $300 fine plus court costs and agrees to leave the state." Opperman and Ragetty were left speechless by the news.

* * *

Inmate no. 0386215 was processed out of the Tarrant County Jail less than 24 hours after appearing in Tarrant County District Criminal Court before the Honorable Judge Harold G. Blackmon III. Judge Blackmon somewhat begrudgingly accepted the plea arrangement recommended by the District Attorney's Office and released Holloway on the pledge that he leave Texas within 48 hours. After reciting all the charges against Holloway and reading through the conditions of the plea deal, Judge Blackmon spoke directly to the defendant. He told Holloway that he was a lucky man to be given a second chance given the seriousness of the charges against him. He admonished Holloway to re-examine his life and start making better choices, starting with committing himself to an accredited rehab program. The judge closed with the stern warning that if Joe didn't change his ways he would be, in effect, putting a gun to his head and pulling the trigger. But at that moment, it wasn't his own head Holloway was planning to put a gun to.

Using some of the $2,000 his mother had wired to him, Holloway caught a cab outside the corrections center in Fort Worth and rode to the airport. With the ticket from his brother in hand, he made straight for the first bar he could find inside Terminal A and downed four shots of vodka straight-up before boarding an American Airlines flight to Tampa. As soon as the plane was airborne, he reached up and pushed the call button to order two more vodkas and was quite annoyed to be told it would be a few minutes before the crew began beverage service. He slumped back in his seat without noticing the two plainclothes Texas Corporate Protection officers sitting directly behind him.

After deplaning in Tampa, Holloway and his two shadows headed directly to Krazy Ray's Kat House, a sleazy strip club just off Memorial Highway that would become his home for the next several days.

* * *

Ragetty made the trip to Granbury to explain the new security arrangements to Sonny and Joan. He glossed over Korman pulling the plug on their protection and simply talked about moving the security plan to the "next phase." At the end of the week, the family would be moving back home, where Texas Corporate Protection would have two security guards in the house round the clock. One would be assigned to travel with Sonny if he had to go into the office or with Joan if she went shopping, and one would remain at the house at all times. Shift changes would be staggered and overlapped so that three officers would be there often.

Wren would receive assignments once a week from her teacher and would soon be back on track at school. Logan could go to soccer practice and games, but one of Ragetty's boys would drive the family everywhere they went. Ragetty offered the encouragement that Holloway had left the state and things would be getting back as close to normal as possible for a family being stalked by a determined lunatic.

Despite the seriousness of the situation, Sonny was determined not to let Holloway paralyze him with fear. His calm exterior masked the inner turmoil he felt every day. He put up a strong front for his family, but as the ordeal dragged on, he began to feel the pressure. He spent a lot of time imagining how he would react if Holloway confronted him, and tossed in his sleep from dreaming of horrific gun battles.

Talking with Ragetty, Sonny confided that he had a great foreboding about the outcome of the dangerous game being played.

"I know Holloway has the upper hand, John," Sonny said. "We have to guess what he is going to do, and we can't be wrong, ever. Eventually someone will drop the ball, or we'll fail to anticipate something, and he will get to me. I'm not saying your guys will be at fault. I'm just being realistic. Somewhere, sometime, Holloway will get to me. I tell everyone I'll be ready, but the truth is, if he catches me off-guard, I'm a dead man. It won't be your fault, John. It will just be how the ball bounced. But regardless of that, I'll be road kill."

Ragetty listened, and he sighed slowly before answering. "Look, Sonny, we've got you covered," he said. "Holloway is the one who will make the mistake. He's a drunk, a doper and a paranoid nut case. If he comes for you, we'll be ..."

"When he comes for me, John, when he comes," Sonny interrupted. Both men were quiet for a minute. Then Sonny asked a much more personal question. "John," he said, "we don't have any family here. Joan has her hands full with the kids. If something happens to me, will you make sure she's OK? She'll need someone local she can trust dealing with Omniplex's attorneys. Promise me you'll help her."

John knew Sonny was hurting, and he choked up. "You can count on me, Sonny," he said. "But it won't come to that.

"I promise you, it will never come to that."

* * *

Once back home, "normal" for the Grahams was a different normal. Two armed guards sitting in the living room 24 hours a day might be reassuring, but it wasn't "normal."

Ragetty had schooled the family on their new reality. It was a lengthy orientation. He walked them through the various escape routes that had been established in the house by the guards and hiked them to the rally point in the park down the street where they were all to meet if they had to leave the home separately. They rearranged furniture for a quick, unobstructed exit from the house and taped poster board over the clear undraped windows next to the front door so no one could look in or shoot through the window from across the street. Sonny and Joan were shown where shotguns were stashed: on top of the hutch in the dining room, by the refrigerator in the

222

kitchen, under the bed in the master bedroom and behind the upright piano in the parlor. Emergency phone numbers in big bold letters were placed next to every phone in the house.

The last training session was just for Sonny. Ragetty knew that Sonny understood the military's killing-zone tactic — the optimal place to attack an enemy —because of his military police training. But Ragetty still walked Sonny from room to room and discussed firing angles with him. It was important to know the best place to take a shot before shooting. Plan a path before retreating was Ragetty's policy.

Ragetty's agents had plotted firing lanes in each of the downstairs rooms to reduce the chance of hitting someone other than Holloway with a stray or ricocheting bullet. Consideration was given to the thickness of walls and the placement of doors and windows. The central theme of the lesson was that if caught off guard, Sonny should shoot when he could, but given a little time, he should take the opportunity to stop an intruder with the best kill shot available.

The last thing Ragetty asked Sonny about was his state of mind. Looking Sonny squarely in the eyes, Ragetty asked, "Could you actually pull the trigger?"

Sonny had been in the Army, it was true, though that didn't mean he could shoot Holloway if he needed to. But Sonny said without hesitation, "Yes, and I wouldn't wait for him to shoot first."

"What would you do if you opened the door and Joe was standing on the porch?" Ragetty asked.

"I would shoot him where he stood and pull his body into the foyer," Sonny coldly said. Ragetty grinned at his star pupil.

Ragetty was pleased and told Sonny he had already spoken with Colleyville Police Chief Steel and Tarrant County Sheriff Thompson about scenarios that might play out at the house. Both men privately assured him that as long as the Grahams were in fear of their lives they would have no problem with law enforcement if they were forced to defend themselves. After all, they *were* in Texas, where it was legal to kill someone to protect your life or your property.

As a parting aside when he was ready to leave, Ragetty warned Sonny, "If you have to shoot him, make sure you kill him." Sonny nodded. He had been taught the three-shot rule at the MP academy. Police officers are trained to be willing to use their weapons if they draw them, and to quickly fire three shots to make sure they stop their man. As an MP, Sonny had heard stories of cops who were killed by perpetrators who had been shot only once.

NINETEEN

It was a beautiful spring Saturday in Dallas, with whip-cream clouds rolling across a cornflower-blue sky. As an orange sun rose above the horizon, the temperature ran into the mid-70s, and a light wind gently shuffled the blossoms popping out on flowering crabapple trees. It was the perfect day for a field trip. Danny Peters and Big Mike were following Joan's van in a gray sedan as the caravan headed to a small town about an hour south of Fort Worth. Wren and Logan were ecstatic because the family was going to the MacDonnal German Shepherd Ranch to pick out a family pet.

The children didn't know the real reason for the trip. To them a new dog would be a friendly playmate, but the animal also would be another line of defense to protect the family from Joe Holloway. The dog could be killed protecting the family, but it might provide the family with a few extra moments to escape or prepare to fight if Holloway showed up at their home.

John Ragetty had suggested buying a German shepherd because they were strong, smart, easy to train and obedient. Police and the military preferred them for search-and-rescue work, and for the Grahams, a well-trained German shepherd would be like adding another guard to the security team.

Ragetty had made arrangements for their dog to be trained in personal protection by the Lone Star Canine Obedience School in Fort Worth. When his firm needed guard dogs they rented them from Lone Star, and John was confident that Lone Star could train any dog the Grahams brought home.

It was Big Mike who had recommended the breeder whose puppies the Grahams were driving to see, but his directions amused Sonny and Joan. With all sincerity, Big Mike told them, "Drive down to near Cleburne and then take the side road south 'til you come to a fork in the road were there is a big old dead tree. Don't turn at that big tree but go on 'til you see another big tree with lots of tall grass growing under it. That's where you turn. After that, drive 'til you see a dirt road and turn in there 'cause that's the dog ranch." Despite Big Mike's meticulous instructions, Sonny called the dog ranch and got the actual location from the owner. But driving down State Road 174 out of Cleburne, they did see a big, old dead tree at a fork in the road and realized they probably could have reached the breeder just as easily following Mike's directions.

Blum was a worn-out town of a hundred residents. Downtown was a two-pump gas station, the police department, Millie's Cafe and a mom-and-pop general store. The German shepherd ranch was a couple miles beyond the city limits down a dirt road, nestled on a grassy tract of farmland surrounded by an eight-foot chain-link fence. The owners, Helen and Butch MacDonnal, had been supplying working dogs to police departments and security companies across the country for more than twenty years.

Through the front gate, the first building the Grahams came to was an old barn that served as an office, warehouse and visitor center. Beyond the barn, identical buildings housed separate kennels, each for a different group of shepherds, females to the left, males to the right. Females with newborn pups were in a separate building, as were females in heat.

Weaned puppies had their own kennel, as did injured, sick and old dogs. There were more than a hundred German shepherds on the property.

The dogs were majestic, large with shiny coats. Some of the males weighed more than a hundred pounds and were nearly six feet tall when they stood on their hind legs. From a distance they all looked the same, but as the kids wandered from cage to cage looking at the puppies, differences became clear. Some were stocky; some were thin; some were gray and black; some were brown and tan. But Wren and Logan thought all of them were cute.

When the kids stopped to look at a group of older pups, they laughed out loud as they watched the pack running around in circles barking at nothing. A certain little fuzz ball caught their attention.

Set apart from the rest in a separate pen was a little female with the saddest eyes. As the kids drew near, the pup came alive and ran to the fence. To the children, it seemed the little lady was barking, "Pick me! Pick me!" The search for a pet came to an abrupt end.

Mrs. MacDonnal explained that a family had bought the puppy, then discovered that their little girl was seriously allergic to dog hair. When the puppy had been returned, she was placed in quarantine to make sure she didn't bring back any diseases to the kennel and had been caged all alone for almost two weeks. Wren and Logan didn't care why their new little friend had been returned because she was so cute. When Mrs. MacDonnal let the pup out of its cage, she ran straight over to Sonny, grabbed a shoelace in her mouth and pulled. The kids were delighted. Soon they were running around a grassy field chasing the frisky puppy. Ten minutes later, they were choosing a name. Logan lobbied for Mickey Mouse; Wren preferred Diamond.

Mrs. MacDonnal told them the dog was a fully pedigreed German Shepherd with a famous lineage. The grandfather, a world-class police dog, was named Rambo and had been featured in dog magazines and law enforcement journals. Mrs. MacDonnal showed the family a picture that had appeared in *Lawman* magazine of Rambo pulling a hapless criminal out the window of a truck.

The father, Sunset Rambo, was huge and also had won acclaim as a working police dog. Sunset Rambo had appeared on the cover of *Security Today*, a national magazine. The mother, Dame Clover, had produced a long line of show dogs that had won many awards. Mrs. MacDonnal told the children they had made a very good choice.

On the way home, the name-the-dog contest continued. Logan offered Soccer and Pal. Wren placed Crystal and Goldie on the list. Sonny told them that because the dog was a purebred and a pedigreed animal, whichever name they chose would be registered with the American Kennel Club, so the dog's name had to be unique among registered dogs. The next day, the family stopped by the Colleyville library and spent an hour researching German titles, names and action words. After much deliberation they settled on Dame Zena of Colleyville. The kids helped Sonny fill out the U.S. Kennel Club's registration form. Sitting at their feet, Zena wagged her tail in approval of her new name.

* * *

John Ragetty picked up a phone call from Colleyville's Detective Mortan. They had been regularly communicating about Holloway, and Mortan was calling with disturbing news. Colleyville police had just been alerted by their Texas Ranger contact that Melissa Holloway's New Orleans divorce attorney, Grover Wilcox, had been found dead in his law office. The crime scene had been staged to look like a suicide, with a scrawled suicide note that was barely legible; however, the death was being ruled a homicide because suicides rarely shoot themselves three times. But Ragetty knew Holloway was being tailed in Tampa by two of his men. It seemed like quite a coincidence, but he told Mortan that Holloway couldn't have been Wilcox's killer.

No more than forty-five minutes later, Ragetty received a second disturbing phone call, this one from the undercover team he had hired to trail Holloway in Tampa. Sometime during the past 48 hours, Holloway had slipped out of his fleabag motel and disappeared. The agents had hoped Holloway would return to the motel, so they had kept a two-day vigil there before deciding they had to alert Ragetty. By then Holloway was gone, and the security agents hadn't seen him in more than thirty hours.

Furious, Ragetty slammed the phone receiver so hard the plastic hand piece cracked. How in the hell could two professionals wait so long to tell him they had lost Holloway? He called Mortan and told the detective he'd been wrong. He had no idea where Holloway was.

He probably wasn't in Tampa. He probably wasn't even in Florida.

* * *

Sonny thought it was good for his family to be back home, but he worried about the possibility of being at the epicenter of a shootout there. He began to think about what the family would do if Omniplex pulled the plug on their security detail. Ragetty had been hinting that Opperman was at odds with Korman and Tyler over the cost of security, and he knew

Omniplex was cutting back. He would have to take some initiative to fill the holes being punched in their security shield.

Soon, he might even have to provide security for his family all by himself.

Sonny arranged to upgrade his home's alarm system, which featured only a control panel in the storage room, keypads at the front and back doors, sensors on the exterior doors and a loud horn in the attic. The new system had an advanced master-control unit that would automatically dial the police if activated, two super loud sirens — one that could not be disconnected by cutting the wires — and several one-touch panic buttons inside the house. Pressure-sensitive pads were laid under the carpet in the hallways, stairway and just inside every door. Shatter detectors were placed on all the windows, and alarms were connected to the two garage doors. Night-sensitive outdoor cameras were mounted on the roof edge to provide a view of the perimeter of the house. The camera network was wired to video recorders and monitors inside the house, and the video from any camera could be enlarged, frozen or replayed.

Next, Sonny called Colleyville Electric and had high-intensity halogen lights installed around the outside. Four industrial-strength fixtures were placed on the ground across the front of the house, and a dual fixture was placed in each corner under the eaves.

With a flick of a switch, the entire outside of the home could be bathed in a bright white light.

Finally, Sonny called a locksmith to rekey all the doors and install deadbolts, and a commercial-grade security brace was placed on the safe room door in the attic.

* * *

The kids were playing in the upstairs game room, and Joan had heard something about making a fort. Whatever they were doing was fine with her. She had laundry to do, and when the kids got along, they were out of her hair.

As Joan came out of the master bedroom with her arms full of dirty clothes, she still felt uncomfortable to find two large uniformed men sitting in the living room. Big Mike and Hoppy were on the day shift today, and they were watching Jerry Springer on TV. The television had been on constantly since Ragetty first knocked on their front door.

Joan appreciated the security the armed guards provided, but having two burly men sitting in the center of her home every minute of every day was getting old. And she was annoyed and unnerved at hearing the TV through the wall between the bedroom and the family room at night. She and Sonny hadn't been intimate since Holloway had appeared in Colleyville.

The two upholstered Lay-Z-Boy chairs the guards used had been subjected to years' worth of wear in the past three months. Her expensive wooden kitchen table bore gouge marks from rifle-cleaning sessions, and the doorframes were beginning to show marks caused by brushes with flashlights and pistols. The beige family-room carpet was getting a faint gray path tramped by dirty combat boots.

Traffic in her driveway was also becoming a problem. Two guards meant two cars in front of the house all the time. At shift change two more agents arrived with two more cars. The two groups of officers would often talk for an hour or so before the group being relieved finally left the property. For much of the time four cars were parked along the street. Then there was the occasional Colleyville Police patrol car or Tarrant County Sheriff's van that would stop by to chat. Ragetty popped in and out, as did Detective Mortan. Joan had looked out the front door once to discover eight police and security vehicles parked across the front of her house.

All the police traffic had created considerable speculation in the neighborhood about what was going on at 704 Saddlebrook Drive, and rumors flew around bridge clubs and PTA meetings. Joan knew it was going to be difficult for the kids to have playmates over but hadn't thought that Wren and Logan wouldn't be invited to any of their friends' homes, either. It seemed no one wanted to take a chance on getting mixed up in whatever was going on at the Grahams.

Coincidentally, the two houses on both sides of the Grahams' home were up for sale. Prospective buyers would stop at one of the homes, see all the parked vehicles, including several police cars, in the Grahams' driveway, and quickly pull away without ever going inside.

One day, the Realtor trying to sell 702 Saddlebrook braved the gaggle of cops and rang Joan's front doorbell. "What exactly is going on with this property?" she asked bluntly. "Why do you have so many police cars parked in your driveway all the time?" Joan briefly explained that they had an ongoing security issue. The Realtor gasped, "Oh shit, I will never sell that house!"

* * *

It had been another beautiful spring day in Colleyville, with a light, warm breeze blowing under a sunny sky and new green growth edging out the dead brown of winter. As dusk settled over the horizon, the evening started to cool and the wind died down. Lights began to pop on up and down the street.

The Graham family had just finished dinner when Hoppy walked in through the back door and announced that there was a problem.

Hoppy reported that he and Big Mike had been watching a dark-brown Mercury parked just up the street from the Grahams' home for about fifteen minutes. The vehicle matched the description of Holloway's car, and it was pointed toward the house with the driver slunk low in the front seat.

Big Mike stayed outside to keep an eye on the driver while Hoppy came in to call for backup and alert the family. He wanted everyone to move to the safe room because as soon as a Colleyville Police patrol arrived, they were going to pull the driver out of the car.

Sonny and Joan quickly ushered the kids upstairs to a small walk-in storage room off the guest bedroom in the back of the house. The room had a back door that led into the attic, where a rope ladder would provide an escape path from the house if needed. Sonny turned off the light, and everyone sat quietly on the floor in the dark as they had rehearsed.

TWENTY

The Grahams sat in darkness in the storage room for what seemed like several hours but in actuality was less than twenty minutes. Sonny held Logan on his lap, and Wren cuddled close to Joan. They sat next to the door that opened into the attic so that if necessary they could make a run for the escape. The kids would go first, and they knew how to open the attic vent and release the rope ladder. If they had to, they could make their way to the ground by themselves. Joan would follow the kids, and Sonny would bring up the rear, or so he told the family. Only Ragetty knew that Sonny would not be going down the rope ladder; he would stay in the storage room with the shotgun hidden there, waiting on Holloway.

Suddenly they detected movement in the house. There were tense moments as everyone strained to hear even the faintest sound. Then a booming voice wafted to the storage room from the entryway below, and Logan broke the silence, calling out, "It's Big Mike." Mike yelled up to signal the all-clear, but as instructed, Sonny didn't open the door until Big Mike knocked with four quick raps, followed by a delay and three additional raps.

There was a collective sigh of relief as the attic door opened and Big Mike greeted the family with a loud, "All clear." Sonny turned to the kids and with a laugh made a feeble joke about everyone passing the test. Joan picked up on the ploy and quickly reassured the kids that they had played their parts perfectly and should there be a real emergency they would know just what to do.

Entering the kitchen with Big Mike, the family was greeted by Ragetty, Hoppy, Mortan and a couple Colleyville police officers they didn't recognize. Joan took the children to the family room and turned on a Disney tape for them. After checking to make sure they were OK, she rejoined the crowd in the kitchen as Ragetty was proclaiming the event that had just unfolded one for the record books.

Ragetty recounted that his agents and a couple of Colleyville Police officers had crept up on the unsuspecting driver of the brown Mercury. Ragetty laughed as he related the story: "Everyone snuck up on this guy who is just sitting there in his car eating a burrito, and without warning they jerked him out at gun-point. There is a brief scuffle in the street before several of my large guys with bad attitudes forcibly subdued him. It's only after they have this poor schmuck handcuffed face down on the street that they learn that he's a very embarrassed and upset Pinkerton agent. And you know the most amazing thing about this whole incident? After the boys wrestled this guy down and go to put the handcuffs on him, he's still holding on to his burrito. That must've been a very special burrito."

Pinkerton Security, formed in 1850 by Chicago policeman Allan Pinkerton as the Pinkerton National Detective Agency, is a legendary security organization that first provided security for shipments of the national railroad companies. In later years the company branched out into international corporate protection.

The Pinkerton agent was watching a house up the street from the Grahams. An oil company executive in the midst of a nasty divorce had the agent watching his vacant second home because he feared his ex-wife might try to break in and take some of the furnishings.

Everyone but the Grahams and the agent thought the event was hilarious. Sonny asked, "Will there be any negative ramification from roughing this guy up?" Ragetty laughed. "I doubt it," he said. "I promised him two tickets to a Cowboys game."

* * *

Joan needed groceries and household supplies, but it was a hassle arranging the trip. She had to coordinate her movements with Ragetty's men to make sure the house, the kids and she were all covered by security. Everywhere she went, one of the security officers rode along. She joked that she had become the talk of the soccer moms, because every time she dropped Logan off for soccer practice, she was with a different man.

Today would be a quick field trip because she just needed a few things. As she entered the Target Superstore in Hurst, Joan told Hoppy Holtz that he could wait for her in the front of the store. She would only be grabbing a few things and would be right back. She got a shopping cart and made straight for the canned goods in the grocery section; to Joan, shopping was a necessary evil to be concluded as quickly as possible. She zoomed around tossing products in her cart until she caught the stare of a scruffy man in a ratty bomber jacket at the end of the aisle. His long, stringy black hair fell out from under a dirty red baseball cap and hung down across his shoulders. Even with a shaggy beard hiding most of his face, Joan could see that his cheeks were sunken and that there were bags under his eyes. Her first thought was that he didn't look like he belonged in Target at any time, let alone the middle of the afternoon. He appeared to be more of the late-night 7-Eleven type of shopper.

Moving on to paper products, Joan put the man out of her mind until she noticed him again at the end of the next aisle. She was the only one on that row, so this time it hit her that he was clearly staring at her. A sick feeling swept through her, and in a moment of panic she dropped the paper towels she was holding into her cart and quickly started for the front of the store. But as she turned onto the center aisle she almost ran into the stalker as he came around the corner toward her. Joan stopped, frozen with fear as the man in the bomber jacket walked straight at her. She wished she hadn't refused to carry the Glock in her purse like Ragetty and Sonny had wanted.

Standing still, Joan stopped breathing as the creep shouldered up next to her. Leaning toward her as he passed, he mumbled something under his breath that she couldn't completely decipher, but she most assuredly understood that she had just received some type of warning.

Joan found Hoppy standing by the cash registers and quickly explained what had happened. He immediately escorted her to the manager's office, where a quick introduction was made, and the store manager let Hoppy and Joan scan the security cameras for the stalker while he dialed the police. Unfortunately, Joan couldn't find anyone in the building who resembled the creep, who must have slipped out of the store as they had gone to the office.

Later that evening on the phone with Sonny, Ragetty said one of his biggest fears might have come true. Ragetty knew that Holloway had befriended two lowlifes while in jail and had funneled cigarettes to them in what appeared to be an attempt to secure favors. Ragetty's concern was that Joan's encounter at Target was the opening salvo of a harassment campaign directed by Holloway. As a worst case, he might have enlisted a couple of his prison pals to hurt the family for him. Ragetty's job had just gotten exponentially more difficult.

Shortly after the Target incident, Sonny started getting threatening phone calls. Usually the caller would growl that Sonny was a dead man, or would soon die, or some other nonspecific intimidation. Sonny taped most of the calls and turned them over to Texas Corporate Protection, but they weren't able to make much out of them. They did, however, discern that more than one person had made the calls, as two different inflections in the pronunciation of Sonny's name could be heard on the recordings. Then, just as suddenly as the calls began, they stopped.

* * *

Sonny, Ragetty and Danny Peters carpooled to downtown Fort Worth for an important meeting at the Water Gardens Business Complex. The Water Gardens, built in 1974, were on the south end of the business district next to the Fort Worth Convention Center. The historic tourist attraction spread out over four acres of prime real estate and contained multiple water features, but the main attraction was an active pool with water cascading forty feet down multiple levels into a smaller recirculating pool at the bottom. The water gardens were designed so people could walk down a series of terraced steps and experience the power, sounds and motion of water crashing around them. On a hot summer afternoon, the gardens would be filled with schoolchildren and tourists enjoying the cool mist of the waterfalls.

At the south end of the gardens stood a modern multistory office building that housed a variety of governmental bureaus, law offices and city departments. Texas Corporate Protection had a suite of rich-looking offices in the building, as did several law-enforcement agencies. The meeting the three men would be attending was not at Ragetty's offices but rather in the Fort Worth headquarters of the famed Texas Rangers.

The Texas Ranger Division, or more simply the Texas Rangers, is the only law-enforcement agency with statewide jurisdiction in Texas. Based in the capital city of Austin, the Rangers have offices in every major city in the state. Stephen F. Austin unofficially created the Texas Rangers in 1823 with a call-to-arms at the outbreak of the rebellion against Mexico. Ten years later, a resolution was introduced in the state legislature creating a permanent body of rangers to protect the Texas border. From that humble beginning the agency grew to its legendary status in the international law-enforcement community. The 150 officers of the Texas Rangers comprise the oldest statewide law-enforcement agency in the United States.

Sitting in the Rangers' large conference room, Sonny was awestruck by the extraordinary photos on the wall and the notable law enforcement presence in the room. As the meeting's host, a Ranger wearing the traditional white Western-style shirt and ten-gallon cowboy hat, introduced the individuals in the crowded meeting room, Sonny heard set after set of initials.

Present were agents from the Federal Bureau of

Investigation (FBI); the U.S. Marshals Service (USMS); the Bureau of Alcohol, Tobacco, Firearms and Explosives (ATF); and the U.S. Drug Enforcement Administration (DEA). Also present were representatives of the U.S. Postal Police (USPP) and the Internal Revenue Service Criminal Investigation Division (IRS-CI). Rounding out the attendees were officers from the Fort Worth, Dallas and Colleyville police departments; the Tarrant and Dallas Country sheriff's departments, and the Dallas-Fort Worth International Airport Police. There were more uniforms in the room than at a military parade. The subject of the meeting was Joseph Vincent Holloway.

Ragetty hadn't given Sonny much background on the purpose of the meeting other than it would have to do with Holloway. It was not until the Ranger at the podium introduced Sonny that he realized he would be part of the program. The meeting began with a general background report on Holloway that included all his vital statistics and a brief timeline of his history. Copies of his resume were handed out to the group, and an overhead projector displayed the same photos that were reproduced on glossy paper in packets distributed to everyone in the room. There were various photos of Joe with his family, his high school graduation picture, a snapshot from an Omniplex award banquet, and the Colleyville and

Tarrant County mug shots.

The agencies and departments already working the Holloway case provided a brief report on why they were interested in Joe. As Sonny listened, he was shocked to learn the degree of illegal activities in which Holloway was involved. The list included murder, attempted murder, criminal aggravated assault, illegal sale of fire arms and ammunition, illegal importation of firearms, the distribution and sale of controlled substances, money laundering, mail and wire fraud, tax fraud, and on and on. By the end of the presentations, Sonny was left with his mouth agape and shaking his head. It was unfathomable to him that he knew and had worked with anyone who was so depraved.

The Texas Ranger in charge of the Holloway files summed up the charges filed against him in Tarrant County and reviewed the status of his case. He concluded by saying, "While we don't have a lot of tangible intel on this guy, it is clear from the comments made here today that he is a walking time bomb and a real public threat. He most certainly needs to remain on our watch list. Any new information that you acquire about his activities should be immediately shared with the rest of this task force. Next on the agenda is Sonny Graham from the Omniplex Corporation, who was Holloway's last boss and the target of his most recent criminal activity.

Sonny is here to help educate us on the events that led to Holloway's recent arrest."

At this point the moderator introduced Sonny and asked him to give the group a brief overview of what had transpired at Omniplex and his dealings with Holloway. The group was especially interested in learning of his mannerisms, quirks, likes and dislikes, and habits that might help them find him. Sonny spoke for about fifteen minutes and fielded questions, then Ragetty signaled it was time to leave as the moderator announced that the next topic would involve highly classified information.

A MOST DETERMINED LUNATIC

TWENTY-ONE

Holloway had no great difficulty slipping the two private eyes Ragetty had hired to tail him in Tampa. He checked into the Camelot Motel on Memorial Highway near the airport under the name Vernon Joseph and told the desk clerk he would be staying for two to three weeks, just in case someone checked on his reservation. He requested a first-floor room in the back of the building, paid for one night in advance, then made sure the boys in the nondescript gray sedan parked across the street saw him head to his room. Joe waited about two hours before he knocked out the window in the bathroom and climbed into the alley. The rented Ford he ordered and prepaid for a week of local use was parked about a block away in the municipal parking lot, and the keys were under the floor mat just as he had instructed. He was good to go.

Once free of his shadows, Joe drove to Route 600 and headed north. He thought anyone looking for him would probably figure he would travel on interstates to cover ground as quickly as possible so he planned to drive old state roads and back ways, hoping to avoid trouble. He stayed on Route 600 until it became 580N at Hillsborough Avenue. He followed 580N until it ended at Route 587. After a short stretch, 587 joined U.S. 19, where Joe turned northwest and eased along the highway through Hudson and North Weeki Wachee until 19 finally merged with U.S. 98.

In Homosassa Springs he stopped to gas up and buy more booze, then he was back on the road cruising through Crystal River, Inglis and Gulf Hammock. He turned north onto U.S. 27 at Perry and drove to just south of Tallahassee before pulling into a Hampton Inn, where he registered this time with the name J. D. Vernon. For dinner he bought a bucket of Kentucky Fried Chicken from the drive-thru across the street from the motel and washed it down with a fifth of vodka. Joe passed out dead drunk before the sun went down.

The following morning, Holloway grabbed a handful of donuts and a carton of orange juice from the complimentary breakfast bar at the Hampton Inn and headed to his car. Before pulling back out onto

U.S. 27, he poured out two-thirds of the orange juice and filled the carton to the top with vodka. On the move again, Joe took back roads running west parallel to Interstate 10 until he again merged back onto Route 90 at De Funiak Springs, Florida. By Spanish Fort, Mississippi, east of Biloxi, he was too drunk to continue, so he parked in a Wal-Mart Super Center parking lot and slept off the booze in the back seat of the rental that was now fast approaching the return date in Florida, soon to be presumed stolen.

Back on the road the next morning, Joe motored through Gulfport, then just west of Bay St. Louis he dropped down to rejoin Route 90 to New Orleans. Until this point he had been cautious, playing it cagey in case he was followed. Even in his inebriated state he was careful to drive the speed limit and obey most of the traffic laws, but now less than an hour from the Big Easy, he became bolder as he neared his old stomping grounds. He threw caution out the window and drove faster. Tonight, he would bivouac with his Brothers of the Red X in the swamp.

* * *

After several months co-existing with their armed house guests, Sonny and particularly Joan started to sour on the live-in security arrangements. They never truly had a moment to themselves, even when they escaped to the privacy of their first-floor bedroom. They always knew that two men were sitting just on the other side of the wall in the living room.

Little things became big irritants. Joan felt uncomfortable popping out of bed in the morning in her pajamas and heading to the kitchen for a cup of coffee. Every morning she got fully dressed before she would walk past the guards on her way to start her day. The guards tried to be invisible, but they always seemed to be in the way, and they tried to be helpful but usually made things more difficult. Joan thought it was great that Hoppy offered to take Zena out in the morning, until the pup started having stomach problems. She discovered that Hoppy had misunderstood the meaning of "dog treat" and was giving the animal a handful of chocolate each time Zena went out.

The housing issue came to a head one day when Joan was trying to make dinner with four guards sitting at the kitchen table drinking coffee. It was shift change, and the two groups of officers were making small talk until Joan had had enough and invited them all to take the conversation outside. That evening she told Sonny they had to do something about the live-ins.

Sonny called Ragetty, who agreed that a realignment of the security arrangement was probably due since they were moving into a longer-range phase. Ragetty asked what Joan would prefer, and Sonny suggested building an addition to the house over the garage to give the security team a headquarters out from underfoot. A staircase on the back of the three-car garage would allow access to the command center without causing continual disruption of the Grahams' home life. Ragetty thought a small annex over the garage could be an ideal spot for his team and said he would run the idea by Omniplex. To his way of thinking, the build-out would cost at most $15,000, small change compared with the enormous cost of the entire operation.

Jericho rejected the idea in a hurry. But Ragetty offered a counter-proposal to park a small mobile trailer on the driveway behind the house that his officers could use as a command post. The trailer would be connected to the house by both audio and video lines providing real-time communication in case of an emergency. The command center would monitor the perimeter of the property round the clock through the video cameras mounted on the outside of the house. Sonny jumped at the opportunity to move their heavily armed friends to a guesthouse in the driveway.

It took Ragetty only a day to move a white fifteen-foot trailer onto the property. Inside there would be enough room for all the necessary weapons, electronics and security guards sitting at a long console. That afternoon Ragetty's technical people were at the house wiring the small command center with phone lines, a bank of video monitors that tapped into the home's camera system, an alarm tied directly into the security system's panic alarm and flood lights on the roof of the trailer that could be activated to provide additional lighting across the back of the house.

Less than 48 hours after the discussion about relocating the security team, the command center in the driveway was up and running. Joan was pleased, even though the guards still had to tramp through her house to use the bathroom.

While Ragetty was discussing the details of the command center with Sonny, he took the opportunity to speak confidentially about the state of affairs at Omniplex. Korman, he told Sonny, had clamped down on the security budget to the point that John wasn't sure how much longer funds would be available.

"Omniplex is going to protect itself at the big New Orleans medical meeting because they really don't have much choice," he said. "The potential that Joe might show up during Gastroenterology Week is so high that it shoots their liability way up. Korman cleared me to fly my boys into town for the meeting. We'll ship all the necessary surveillance equipment and weapons labeled as convention displays by FedEx direct to the hotel. That way we avoid any questions at the airport. We're setting up a command post at the downtown Hilton, and I will have five of my best guys in the company's sales booth in the convention hall during exhibition hours. I'm going to assign a detail to shadow the senior guys — Sid, Mike and Mark — during the convention. We're not telling New Orleans PD that we'll be fully armed because it will complicate things too much. I have some friends over there who can help if we need to explain things to the locals."

Ragetty paused, thinking how to continue. After a few seconds, his tone softened. "Sonny," he said, "I hate to tell you this, but I fear the Omniplex checkbook is about to close. Korman is a penny-pinching little prick who's only concerned about covering his own ass. I don't think we can count on him funding this show much longer." He reassured Sonny that Opperman was still covertly supplementing the cost of the protection, but added, "Mike's funds have limits too. I'm guessing they're probably nearly exhausted."

Sonny thought for a second. "Do you think the company would be willing to negotiate some sort of buyout on their liability?" he asked. Ragetty shrugged. "Hell, at this point I honestly have no idea what Korman will do," he said.

Undaunted, Sonny continued. "I'm thinking about offering Omniplex a waiver of liability in exchange for a lump sum that would allow me to leave the company and relocate my family. If Omniplex agrees, I would be willing to sign a waiver to accept responsibility for protecting my family going forward and have no legal hold on Omniplex in the future. But they would have to cough up enough dough to at least give me a fighting chance to protect my family and compensate me for the terrible situation they've put me in. Their inability to deal with Joe Holloway put me in this position. Money can't undo the damage," he said. "But it sure will help."

Ragetty thought about the proposal and asked, "How much do you think it would take for you to agree to a buyout?" Sonny had already discussed it with Joan and had a figure in mind. He shot back a number that at first made Ragetty flinch. "Tell that son-of-a-bitch Korman that it will take at least a seven-figure offer to start a discussion," Sonny said. He wanted to leave himself some negotiating room because he expected Sid Korman would counter with an unrealistic lowball figure. Ragetty let out a low slow whistle, but after thinking about it, he realized that Sonny's target amount wasn't outrageous.

Mike Opperman had briefed Ragetty on Sonny's confidential corporate and personal history when he took the job, so Ragetty knew that Sonny earned more than $200,000 a year plus benefits, perks and bonuses. Given his rising star with the company and his young age, it was conceivable that he could continue to expand his compensation for the next ten or fifteen years.

But if the Grahams agreed to go it on their own they would be eating the cost of relocation and whatever security the family hired in the future. Sonny would have to start his career over in a new industry to make it difficult for Holloway to find him. Considering everything Sonny would be giving up, the risk that he would be assuming for the future, and the savings Omniplex might realize if there were a lawsuit, in Ragetty's mind a million-dollar settlement shouldn't be out of the question.

Ragetty asked Sonny whether he wanted him to put the buyout proposal in play with Omniplex. Sonny and Joan were growing tired of being sitting ducks for Holloway, and they knew that Omniplex's purse would run dry. The buyout seemed to be the logical solution. Sonny was reluctant to negotiate directly with Omniplex and wouldn't speak with them about it until he had hired a lawyer, but he wanted to know what the company thought about such a proposal. Ragetty said he would run the proposal up the flagpole and see whether anyone in Jericho saluted.

But that idea lasted as long as talk of an addition over the garage. Korman rejected the idea out of hand.

However, after the conference call with Korman, Opperman and Tyler, Opperman had called Ragetty back to float a counter-proposition. Opperman suggested that he might be able to sell Korman on relocating the Grahams to England.

The company could treat the move as a corporate relocation, covering most of the cost, and Sonny could work for the Omniplex affiliate in Southend-on-Sea, Essex, in the United Kingdom. Southend-on-Sea was a seaside resort town on the north side of the Thames about forty miles east of central London and home to the longest leisure pier in the world. A city of 100,000, the upscale community was the corporate home and primary manufacturing location for a medical products accessory company owned by Omniplex Worldwide.

One night after dinner and after the kids had been put to bed, Sonny brought up the possibility of a relocation. "What do you think about moving?" he asked Joan. "I think it is inevitable that unless Holloway is put in prison for life or killed, we'll be on our own." Joan made no attempt to respond so Sonny trudged forward with a one-sided conversation and offered places to move. Albuquerque, New Mexico. Fort Collins, Colorado. Spokane, Washington. Joan nodded as if to say, "If you think so," but the look on her face said, "I am not moving."

Undeterred, Sonny continued, "We would need to find a city big enough to provide us with a comfortable lifestyle but out of the way enough that we could basically disappear." Finally, Joan spoke in a slow, low voice. "I have no interest in living in Albuquerque, New Mexico. Or any other backwater. I refuse to let a crazy man drive me out of my own home." Sonny realized that moving out of the country wasn't going to fly, either, but he decided to take a chance.

"Okay, Albuquerque is out, but what about moving to England? That might be an interesting opportunity. We could travel the continent, and the kids could get a first-hand international education."

Joan answered slowly. "How long do you think we'd have to stay there?" she asked. Sonny wanted to lie and tell her it would probably just be for eight or ten months because Holloway would certainly be arrested and jailed within a year. But he thought the truth was much more bleak and decided there was nothing to be gained by trying to finesse his wife. "Over a dozen law enforcement agencies have an interest in him, but no one has a clue where he is," Sonny said. "He could show up anywhere at anytime. Or worse, he might never show up and simply remain a shadowy threat. We might be gone for a long time."

The last scenario was profoundly disturbing. Holloway might drink himself to death in the swamp or be killed in a gun or drug deal gone bad down in the delta, and no one would ever know. There was the possibility the Grahams might be looking over their shoulders for a decade or more. Sonny wasn't sure how long the family could endure the pressure of the unknown or what toll the situation would take on the kids, or his marriage.

The more he thought about the long-term ramifications of the ordeal, the sadder it made him. He had brought this all down on the family. Suddenly he blurted out, "I should have played it safe and taken my own sweet time dealing with Joe, no matter how much damage he caused. But no, I had to bail the company out and do what was right for the business. I was a fool. I should have anticipated the complications."

Sonny continued. Why had he always been the one sticking his neck out? In executive meetings, he was always the one who told Jericho what it needed to hear. Others would clam up, pass the buck, equivocate, dodge. Sonny didn't do that. If he thought something needed to be done, he got it done. If something needed to be said, he said it. "But look where all that team spirit has left me," he said to Joan. "I'm the one Holloway is gunning for, not Korman."

Joan knew Sonny was hurting and had been silently carrying the weight of the ordeal on his shoulders. She leaned over and touched his hand.

"Michael Opperman respects you for that, and Mark Tyler fears you because of it," she told him in a soothing voice. But Sonny knew his straight-shooting manner and company-first attitude had put his family in harm's way. He wasn't sure he'd be able to forgive himself if anything happened to them.

A MOST DETERMINED LUNATIC

TWENTY-TWO

Joe vegetated with the Brothers of the Red X in their bayou encampment for a week drinking vodka, snorting cocaine and punching prostitutes. Most of the time he was so completely inebriated that even the other drunks left him alone. The more cocaine he blew, the more paranoid he became. After awhile he had convinced himself that the whole world was against him, and that Omniplex in general, and Sonny Graham specifically, were the two primary causes of his trouble. However, there was also a supporting cast of other troublemakers who had contributed to his decline and also needed to be punished. There was Melissa's divorce attorney, for one, and the Omniplex interloper who had taken over his old sales territory.

There was plenty of time to deal with them all. A lot of people would pay for turning against him.

Joe planned to repay Omniplex first with a special New Orleans Convention Center extravaganza at the end of the week. He had gone over the plan in his mind a hundred times, and the mission had been conceived well before he torched his Destrehan home and set out on the road to settle scores. It had been refined to perfection as he crisscrossed the county stacking his various targets and preparing for battle. Now he was ready for combat. Thanks to his Red X brothers, he had a fresh stash of weapons and ammo purchased with his mother's life savings.

Joe could see the plan unfolding in his mind's eye as clearly as if it were reality, though in his delusions everything moved slowly, deliberately. He had no interference and more than ample time to move from one phase to another. He could clearly see himself pulling up to the loading dock behind the convention center. He had been there many times for regional and national medical meetings so he knew just where to park and exactly how to find the person he needed to see. He would bribe the union dock supervisor to let him carry a large duffle bag across the loading dock and onto the exhibit floor. No one would ask to check inside the duffle because he was well known in New Orleans as an important medical equipment salesman. Dock personnel and security would think he was attending the meeting and bringing in display equipment to set up at a company booth. If someone did question him, he would simply buy them off with a Ben Franklin or two, whatever it took to get them to look the other way.

Once inside the exhibit hall he would make his way to the secured door that closed off the staircase to the catwalk at the top of the convention center. A large bolt-cutter concealed in the duffle bag would make short work of the padlock on the metal safety door. The catwalk would afford him an unobstructed view of the massive Omniplex booth in the center of the exhibit hall below.

Omniplex would be the meeting's largest exhibitor, so he would know right where to find them. He wouldn't be bothered on the catwalk because before climbing up he would slide on coveralls sporting a large patch of the International Brotherhood of Electrical Workers Local Union 130. Anyone who saw him would take for granted that he was working on the lighting.

Timing was everything, so it would be of critical importance to make his move to the catwalk just after the exhibit hall opened in the morning. Omniplex would have more than fifty personnel attending the show, and they would be required to be in the 2,000-square-foot sales booth waiting to greet the morning rush of doctors. Joe had worked enough meetings to know that the busiest time at a medical meeting would be the first day of technical exhibits right after the doors to the exhibit halls swung open in the morning.

Doctors generally wanted to meander through the maze of corporate exhibits in the morning so they could be out of the hall before noon. In the afternoon many physicians would attend seminars and breakout groups to learn more about the latest research or newest procedures. A few would opt out of the meeting to take their private scrub nurse to lunch and then shopping at Maison Blanche on Canal Street for something special to wear for an intimate dinner that evening at Commander's Palace, Antoine's or Galatoire's. New Orleans was a popular meeting destination for doctors who had more than medicine on their mind.

Holloway could see himself on the catwalk opening the duffle bag and taking out one of four high-powered, specially modified AK-47s concealed in the large tote. He had purchased the automatic rifles, along with several handguns and a couple knives, while in the bayou. All the munitions had been smuggled into the country from China, then modified by the Brothers of the Red X.

Joe dreamed of waiting for just the right minute when the maximum number of people were in the Omniplex sales booth, then standing up on the catwalk and throwing several smoke bombs to the floor below. As the smoke bombs exploded, panic would break out in the convention hall, and people would begin running for the exits, where they would create a bottleneck at the narrow doorways.

Then, and only then, Joe Holloway would reap his revenge on Omniplex. He would run up and down the catwalk and empty clip after clip of high-velocity rounds into the screaming crowd. At this point in his fantasy he would smile as he took a moment to survey the carnage he had inflicted on Omniplex. It would be like shooting fish in a barrel.

In the last scene of his vision, Joe would escape from the building across the loading dock during the confusion that followed the massacre. He would shoot any dockworkers, security guards or police officers who got in his way.

Holloway was ready to launch his payback tour. He had the plan, the weapons, the hit list and the skill to execute the plan. He was ready to die and take as many people with him as possible.

If only he had not been so falling-down drunk.

* * *

After a weeklong bender Holloway finally sobered up enough to check his equipment, pack the car and hit the road. He had plenty of time to get to the meeting. He drove into New Orleans and went straight to the convention center. Just as planned, he located a secluded parking spot behind the loading dock among the semi-trailers that carried exhibit equipment to the meeting. He parked and retrieved the duffle bag from the trunk, but his gait was a little wobbly as he headed to the loading dock platform. He had been plastered on booze and cocaine so long that the residual effects markedly impaired his mobility, but he managed to make it up the steps to the dock and find the supervisor's office. He told the union boss that he was with Omniplex Worldwide and had a delivery of important equipment for their booth. He needed to be cleared into the meeting hall immediately so he could get the instruments to their booth before the meeting opened. He offered the dock master $200 cash.

The union boss who controlled the loading dock was Carlton de la Grand, a gruff little man with a ratty mustache and a nasty disposition. Nothing happened on the receiving ramp unless Carl said it could. He had been the union's lead dog at the convention hall for more than a dozen years and had taken bribes from hundreds of companies to expedite unloading, facilitate trailer parking, find mysteriously lost equipment and allow unregistered convention attendees in the back door without an ID badge. So it was no big deal when Holloway flashed two crisp hundred-dollar bills in Carl's face as his ticket into the meeting.

But unexpectedly, Carl balked. He dipped his head and furrowed his brow as if in disbelief. He shook his head from side to side as he spoke in a slow, strong Cajun drawl and informed Holloway that everyone from Omniplex had left the building when their booth was disassembled at the end of the meeting, ten days ago.

Joe was dumbfounded. How could this be? He had a plan. How could he have miscalculated so badly? Carl watched him for a few seconds, then turned back to his business of being difficult and taking bribes. Joe continued to stand on the loading dock trying to make sense of what he had just been told. Finally, he slowly turned and headed back to the car. He reached under the front seat and pulled out a plastic water bottle filled with vodka and a spritzer of cocaine. He needed to get his bearings and regroup.

Sitting in the stolen rental car, Joe kept going over his strategy. Somewhere along the way he had lost track of time. His master plan was in total disarray. But after a few more gulps from the plastic bottle and a couple minutes of reflection, he realized that not everything was lost. All he had to do was adjust the plan to current circumstances. True, he had blown the chance to inflict chaos at the medical meeting, but he knew where Omniplex's corporate office was. He could move ahead with the targets he had on his list, then circle back to Jericho to finish the mission.

* * *

Grover St. Clair Wilcox III, Esq., was an infamous and rich New Orleans divorce attorney. He could regularly be seen on TV tabloid shows championing the cause of one of his wealthy and supposedly browbeaten female clients. Wilcox specialized in rescuing oppressed women who were, in his mind, due large sums of alimony and child support from their filthy rich executive, physician or celebrity husbands.

Wilcox was a character of the first order, with long thick white hair that he greased down and brushed straight back. His lovely locks fell on the shoulders of his expensive custom Savile Row suits. He favored wild ties and monogrammed tailored dress shirts with wide contrasting-color French cuffs. Rather than a conventional briefcase he carried an Italian-made brushed leather over-the-shoulder attaché that bore his initials in bold gold-embossed letters above a large fleur-de-lis.

Wilcox knew his way around a divorce case, having been married and divorced three times himself. He would get caught cheating, pay a hefty settlement to his ex-wife and pledge never to marry again, only to meet another irresistible beauty who would soon be his next ex-wife.

Normally, Wilcox would never have taken Melissa Holloway as a client. She was neither famous nor independently wealthy, and her husband didn't have a seven-figure income for him to tap. Melissa was everything Wilcox tried to avoid as a client. When she entered his office his first thought was, "Oh my, how did this poor plain woman ever get an appointment?" But as she sat in his office and tearfully explained the trauma Joseph Holloway had put her through and the terrible plight he had left her in, he simply could not say "no" to the soft-spoken, mousy little lady. Uncharacteristically, he took pity on her. He would take the case pro bono, he said, filing for a petition of divorce due to mental and physical cruelty. He hugged her as she left the office and told her not to worry, he would handle everything. Besides, he didn't think the process would take a lot of his valuable time, and it felt good to be benevolent to this shell-shocked housewife and mother.

As usual, Wilcox was right. The case was an uncontested exercise that he gave to his second-year associate, Clayton Medcalf. Melissa got her divorce and moved in with her brother, and Wilcox promptly forgot her.

The Wilcox Law Office was just up the Mississippi River from the French Quarter, in the city's Lower Central Business District. Roughly bordered by Canal, Tchoupitoulas, Poydras, O'Keefe, Common and South Saratoga streets, the legendary location had been a center of business since 1825. A high-rent district bustling with professional businesses, department stores, financial institutions, restaurants and specialty shops, the Lower Central Business District was an ideal setting for the flamboyant Wilcox. From his 27th-floor suite in the celebrated Bienville Professional Building, he could sit at his 19th Century Louis XV leather-top writing desk and watch tugboats prod coal barges along the Mississippi River.

Wilcox didn't usually arrive at his office until mid-morning because he would meet clients for dinner, then return to the office to work until after midnight. A night owl by nature, the lights in his office would be burning long after the rest of the building went dark. Most nights, after midnight Wilcox would take the executive elevator to his private parking space in the basement, fire up his new Jaguar and head across town to his empty $3.5 million, seven-bedroom, nine-bath, 15,000-square foot home that looked out at the gray-green waters of Bayou St. John.

This night was no different than a hundred other late-night work sessions until Wilcox thought he heard a noise in the corridor outside his office. He listened for a moment, then decided it was nothing and went back to reading the court record on his desk. Then he thought he heard the sound again, this time more distinct, coming from the suite's outer office. As he looked up, he never saw the .45-caliber shell that exploded from the barrel of the Beretta PX4 Storm Pistol pointed at his head. The first bullet reached him before he heard the gun go off. In close succession, two more bullets hit Wilcox in the center of his forehead and blew the back of his skull all over the framed diploma from LSU's law school hanging on the wall behind him. Wilcox was dead before his face hit his expensive antique desk.

* * *

Joe was ready to move. He had cut back on the booze and cocaine to clear his head and get back on plan. His business finished in the Crescent City, he abandoned the rental car on the edge of the French Quarter, leaving the keys in the ignition to ensure it would be stolen in short order. Better to let someone else get arrested for that. He bought a well-used Ford pickup truck in the Ninth Ward from an old-timer whose eyesight was failing so he didn't drive anymore. The elderly gentleman was pleased to accept cash for his asking price and an extra $300 to forgo the paperwork. The rusted, timeworn truck wasn't a showpiece, but it ran, and that was all Joe cared about. No one would be looking for this gray bucket of bolts.

Keeping to his plan of driving along byways rather than the interstates, Joe left New Orleans heading northwest toward Baton Rouge on Route 64. Leaving the "Big Raggedy" as Baton Rouge was known, Joe turned onto Route 71 several miles north of Lafayette, just east of Opelousas. He traveled through Alexandria near the Thistlethwaite State Wildlife Area, where magnificent herds of large deer roam. Joe then merged on to Route 64 along the edge of the Kisatchie National Forest, the Loggy Bayou wildlife preserve and the banks of the Red River. The course took him through Natchitoches and finally into Shreveport, the governmental seat of Caddo Parish.

Shreveport is the third-largest city in Louisiana and was founded in 1836 by the Shreve Town Company, a corporation established to develop a town at the juncture of the newly navigable Red River and the Texas Trail, an overland route into the newly independent Republic of Texas. The city had a rough-and-tumble old river-town reputation and was the perfect stopover for Holloway. A fellow Brothers of the Red X'er who Joe knew from the bayou had moved to Shreveport, so he had a place to get off the road and hunker down for a day or two.

TWENTY-THREE

Claude Delmar was not the brightest bulb in the box, but his live-in girlfriend, Dalotta, a part-time prostitute and full-time crack head, made him seem like Albert Einstein. Together they ran a smoke shop that fronted for a drug den in a back room. Their doublewide mobile home probably should have been condemned by some official government agency for being a public eyesore and health hazard, but nevertheless it served as Holloway's motel for three days. Claude treated Joe to a stash of cocaine in exchange for an unregistered and illegally obtained Colt revolver. The two societal failures spent much of their time together drinking 100-proof vodka, snorting cocaine and entertaining Dalotta in the bedroom. The vodka and cocaine were excellent, Dalotta not so

275

much, as she was too spaced out to perform much of the time.

After three blurry days, Holloway emerged from his substance-abuse haze and left the trashy trailer without saying goodbye, as both Claude and Dalotta were wasted. After a couple tries, the old truck started, and Joe headed out for Tarrant County along with the contents of Claude's billfold and the revolver Joe had given him.

Before leaving town he abandoned the old truck and bought a used metallic-copper-brown 1989 Mercury Grand Marquis for cash. He was going to arrive in Colleyville in style.

Outside Marshall, Texas, he picked up Highway 80 West, and despite being delayed because of a traffic accident, less than three hours later he was on the Airport Expressway just west of Dallas. Holloway found a La Quinta Inn in Hurst, next to the interstate, and checked in under the name Claude Delmar using a credit card he had discovered in the trailer.

Holloway slept for a couple hours, then grabbed dinner from the 7-Eleven next to the motel, enjoying a three-day-old gourmet sandwich from the cold case. Then he tried to call his jail buddy, Nelson Smith, but found that Snuffy's phone had been disconnected.

Next, he tried Lester Newcastle, who answered in a garbled voice after the seventh ring. Weasel was high on crack and could hardly speak. At first he didn't remember Joe, but with some coaching, Weasel recalled that they had served time together in Greenbay. Holloway reminded Weasel that he was owed a favor and made it clear he was calling in his marker. Weasel wasn't all that interested in helping with Joe's project.

Weasel Newcastle grew up in Watauga, Texas, in the Mid-Cities area of Tarrant County, north of Fort Worth. His mother was an actress and stripper who worked nights and slept until noon. When she wasn't pole dancing or taking drugs, she entertained "boyfriends" in her small two-bedroom ranch home while Lester amused himself in the living room. Lester never knew his father, who had been killed during a drunken bar fight before Lester was two years old. Lacking real parents, young Lester was ineffectively raised by his well-meaning but incompetent grandmother, Haddie Clark. Haddie died when Lester was twelve, and he pretty much raised himself after that.

Weasel had been a lousy student but a good football player, so with a little special assistance from his coach he stayed eligible and graduated from high school. But lacking a sufficient grade-point average and any real motivation, high school was the end of his educational pursuits. During the next ten years, a series of dead-end jobs and minor run-ins with the police left him penniless and unemployed. Weasel then got serious about his chosen profession and was busted robbing a warehouse full of electronics.

Two years in the joint toughened him up for a shot at the big time. He had been working on a major score before he met Holloway in Greenbay. Lester masterminded a plot for an armed robbery of a local credit union, but the caper fizzled when he was tossed back in the can for beating his ex-girlfriend to a bloody pulp while in a drunken rage. She knew enough about the robbery plan to rat him out to the authorities, so just after finishing his sentence on the abuse charge, he was hit with a serious criminal indictment.

Weasel really didn't want to do Joe's bidding, given that he was out on bail while awaiting trial, but he changed his mind when Holloway told him he would kill him if he didn't pay his debt. Lester didn't know Joe very well but knew enough about him to believe he meant exactly what he said. So Weasel agreed to meet Joe at the Burger King on Highway 183 in Hurst the next day.

* * *

Ragetty had been summoned to Jericho to meet with Mark Tyler, Michael Opperman and Sidney Korman, along with a special guest appearance by Aaron Silverstein, the corporate attorney. Ragetty had been invited to defend the cost of Texas Corporate Protection's security. After the call from Tyler, Ragetty prepared for the meeting feeling as if he were being hauled before a medieval Inquisition.

As his American Airlines flight touched down on the challengingly short runway at LaGuardia Airport in New York, Ragetty looked out at the water surrounding the landing strip on three sides and like Sonny before him understood why pilots call the airport "the USS LaGuardia." The plane braked to a quick stop, and Ragetty felt that he knew what it must be like to land on an aircraft carrier. A brisk wind was blowing up a storm, causing the gray water to whitecap all across Flushing Bay. Even with wind-chill temperatures in the 20s, the tarmac at LaGuardia was sure to be warmer than the greeting he expected to receive at Omniplex.

The chauffer-driven Lincoln Town Car dropped Ragetty at the main entrance to Omniplex's corporate office, and he was ushered upstairs to the small meeting room across from Opperman's office. Opperman, Tyler and Silverstein were already in the room for the 1 p.m. meeting, but it wouldn't start until Korman decided to make an appearance, which could be anytime in the next half-hour. Meaningless small talk filled the room until Korman walked through the door at 1:37 p.m.

Korman offered no greetings and never acknowledged Ragetty's presence, jumping directly to the meeting's issue: his desire to pull the plug on the security expense for Sonny's family. Korman was suffering from an extreme case of "short man syndrome" and used such situations to inflate his ego. Generally rude, in difficult or tense situations he often became overbearing and profane. This meeting was no exception.

Korman began the meeting with a caustic opening salvo. "I see absolutely no reason to continue pissing away tens of thousands of dollars for an unnecessary protection plan for one man," he said. "Nothing has happened to Sonny Graham, nothing happened during Gastroenterology Week, and nothing is going to happen in the future. Joe Holloway is a bumbling drunk who couldn't fight his way out of a paper sack. I will not allow Omniplex to be intimidated by hollow threats that Graham might take legal action against the company. Likewise, Mr. Ragetty, I will not allow your company to hold us hostage to an unrealistically expensive security scam." Ragetty wanted to jump up from the table and smack Korman silly but instead gritted his teeth and said nothing.

Opperman countered with the same two arguments he had been making since the threat first materialized: The company had too much to lose and could not take a chance that everything would simply turn out OK, and Sonny was a loyal star employee and deserved the company's help. Tyler sat quietly, letting Opperman carry the flag in the battle. He had reassessed the situation and had decided to stay as far out of the fray as possible. If Opperman fought Korman and ended up imploding, he would be the likely beneficiary as long as he didn't end up on Korman's bad side.

Opperman asked Ragetty for a report on the status of the tracking team hunting for Holloway. Ragetty reported that the news was not good. "We lost his trail in Florida and at this time have no idea where he is," he said. "As a result, I terminated the tracking detail to save the expense." Without being asked for his opinion Ragetty continued, "At this point there are only two things that are certain. First, there is one place we can be assured Joe will eventually show up, and that is at the Grahams' home in Colleyville. The problem is, nobody can predict when he will get there. Second, I firmly believe that Holloway will never stop in his attempt to murder Sonny Graham until he is either captured, killed or successful."

Then the shouting began. Korman again accused Ragetty of manipulating the situation to extract a ransom from Omniplex. Ragetty yelled back that he didn't need Omniplex's money and if it weren't for his true concern for the Grahams, he would chuck the entire operation. Opperman accused Korman of putting profits before lives. As the meeting turned into the verbal equivalent of a street brawl, Tyler sat smugly silent.

Korman's bald head turned brilliant red as he screamed at Opperman: "Shut up and listen to me. I run this company, and don't you forget it. I'm the one who answers to the board of directors. Opperman, if you can't get with the program and support me on this, then I suggest you resign right now." Opperman was fuming, his face flush with anger as he shouted back, "Well, Mr. Korman, I'm in charge of a threatened billion-dollar business, which is the life blood of your Omniplex. I will not let you put my operation at risk as a result of your personality flaw that prevents you from having any empathy *what-so-ever* for an at-risk employee. An employee, may I point out, that this company put in harm's way as the result of your decisions." Then Opperman took off the gloves.

In a calm, calculated voice, Opperman told Korman, "If you insist on cancelling the security protection for the Grahams, I will personally see to it that a special session of the board is called to review your handling of this entire situation." Staring down Korman, Opperman flatly challenged his boss to a bet as to whether the board would invite him to appear at such a meeting, then said that Korman of course knew that the board would ask him for a report. Then he sunk the dagger in Sidney's heart. Opperman stood and started for the door but stopped short of leaving the room, turning to address Korman once more: "I guarantee you that if you force me to go to the Board, when I am given the opportunity — and you know that I will be given the opportunity — I will tell them in enlightening detail exactly what you have been up to and the huge gamble you are taking with this corporation's future." At that precise second, Korman blinked. He knew Opperman wasn't bluffing, and he was afraid he had a winning hand.

* * *

In the car on the way back to LaGuardia, Ragetty reflected on the meeting and his elevated respect for Opperman. He had just watched a successful executive put his meteoric career on the line for one of his best employees. Ragetty knew this wasn't something that happened every day in the corporate world. The meeting had also confirmed his low opinion of Tyler and Korman.

As his flight thundered down the runway and quickly banked out over the water of the bay, Ragetty looked out the small window in first class and considered the outcome of the showdown. The positive was that he had a new agreement that allowed him to continue to protect the Grahams at the current security level. And he wasn't being forced to make a decision about abandoning the family, at least not today. The negative was that the contract extension was month-to-month, and given Korman's volatile personality, it could be terminated any moment. Ragetty spent the rest of the flight considering how to use the marginal budget he was working with and how much he should tell Sonny about what happened during the meeting. He decided not to say anything.

TWENTY-FOUR

Holloway went over the plan with Lester again because he still wasn't sure Weasel fully grasped his role. Tomorrow morning, they would meet at the Burger King and drive south to Colleyville. They would park in the Presbyterian church parking lot near the intersection of Sonny's street with Mockingbird Lane. A few minutes apart they would separately walk down the hill to 704 Saddlebrook Drive.

Joe was right: Weasel didn't understand the plan because, one, he was still a bit high after a night of major partying and, two, he was generally just not all that quick on the uptake. This became clear to Joe when Weasel asked why they were going to the house in the daylight. Wouldn't it be better to wait for darkness? They could wear dark clothes and sneak up on the house. Joe looked at his assistant as if the dim-witted Weasel were insane. He slowly explained again that part of the joy of this payback would be seeing Sonny comprehend what was happening and realize that he could do nothing to prevent it. This could only be fully appreciated during the daylight. Showing up in the pitch-black of midnight and ambushing his pray without being seen simply wouldn't work. Weasel stared at Joe like a confused puppy. Holloway hadn't enlightened him with the real reason for going to the house in broad daylight.

Since his ungrateful lying wife left him and was, unbelievably, awarded sole custody of his daughter, Kimberly, he had been completely adrift. Melissa had purposely destroyed his future and sabotaged him financially. Then Sonny, Omniplex's tyrannical troublemaker, singled him out as a scapegoat to cover his own incompetence. Sonny had lied about him and manipulated sales data to make him look bad. He had unfairly gotten Joe fired from the job he was entitled to, a position of importance that he deserved. Adding insult to injury, Omniplex hadn't stood up to Sonny on Joe's behalf and allowed the meddler's lies to go unchallenged. Since he'd been fired, life had lost all meaning for Joe.

What Lester was probably incapable of ever understanding was that Joe was ready to check out and wanted to go in a blaze of glory. He wanted to be remembered as the man who avenged all grievances and righted all wrongs. He would be revered as the man who settled old scores and signed off on his terms. People would be talking about him long after he was gone. He would make sure of it.

In his deluded state, Holloway envisioned walking up to the Grahams' front door and ringing the bell. Sonny would answer the door and see Joe standing on the porch. At that point Sonny would realize that he was going to pay for all his transgressions. He would plead for his life and beg for mercy, admitting that he had purposefully lied. Sonny would cry and tell Joe not to take away the father of two little kids, even though he had helped Melissa steal his daughter. And then, without any sense of guilt or compassion, Joe would shoot Sonny Graham several times in the head and watch him die in the entryway of his home.

If Weasel kept to the script and played his part correctly while Joe was dealing with Sonny, he would break in through the back door and round up Sonny's wife and children. Once inside, Holloway planned to quickly shoot Joan, Wren and Logan. And then he would shoot Weasel, before simply walking away from the house. The plan was perfect, and every time he replayed it in his mind he escaped without interference. What Weasel didn't understand was that he was needed to make sure Sonny's wife and kids didn't escape before they could be executed. Weasel hadn't been told there were multiple targets, including himself.

But Joe didn't really care whether he got away. Once he had accomplished his mission, he was ready to check out. He didn't even care whether he got to everyone on his checklist. Even if he walked from the murder scene at the Grahams' house, he knew the police eventually would intercept him and that the encounter would end in gunfire. He was prepared and ready for the fight. He just wanted to take as many of his enemies and cops with him as possible.

That evening Joe stayed in his room at the motel and drank — a lot. He didn't want to risk having a chance encounter with a policeman that might become a confrontation before he completed his mission. To make sure he stayed awake, about 1:30 in the morning Joe shot a speedball, an intravenous injection of cocaine and heroin. He didn't want to fall asleep and miss the grand opportunity in front of him. He was determined not to let this chance slip through his hands as had happened at the convention in New Orleans. This time, he would be on top of his game.

The next morning, Joe was slow and groggy from the multiple drugs, copious amount of alcohol and all-night vigil. He could barely speak but was able to drive to the Burger King by 9:30 a.m. and promptly drained four cups of coffee. He waited impatiently for nearly an hour before starting to call Lester every couple minutes. The phone rang repeatedly but was never answered. After ten calls Holloway gave up. Weasel wasn't coming. He was furious, but it made no difference. Weasel was a worthless deadbeat and would probably just screw up the mission. At best, he would have been of marginal help. Joe could get the job done himself.

Joe slowly drove toward Colleyville and turned onto the route toward Sonny's home as he'd planned. But at the last minute, rather than park at the church and walk down the hill to Sonny's house, he decided to drive right up to the front door and boldly park in the circular drive. That would make for an even more defining statement and faster getaway. He was delighted with his own tactical flexibility, confident that after the fact, the police and news media would view this on-the-spot adjustment as a brilliant maneuver.

Holloway turned onto Mockingbird Lane and eased down the grade toward Saddlebrook Drive as he had done several times during the past year and a half. Then, halfway down the hill, he jammed on the breaks. What the hell? There were four cop cars in the driveway. Where did these goons all come from? That stupid son-of-a-bitch Weasel must have tipped off the cops. Joe was *pissed,* and he slammed his fist hard on the steering wheel. This was not the way the plan was supposed to work. With so many police at the house there would be no way for him to get to Sonny before the cops got to him. The whole situation was turning out to be a first-rate disaster. First, Snuffy bailed and was a total washout, then Weasel was a no-show, and now cops were at the house. Joe was ready to explode with anger. The plan had turned to crap, and he wasn't sure what to do about it.

What Joe couldn't have known was that it was a shift change at the Grahams' house, and both the outgoing and incoming security details were there. Holloway sat looking at four Texas Corporate Protection company cars thinking they were Colleyville police cruisers. For several minutes, he glared at the cars. His chemically fogged mind cleared enough to realize he had encountered a significant amount of difficulty the last time he stopped and stared at 704 Saddlebrook Drive. He punched the car into gear and rapidly backed up the hill to the nearest driveway to turn around, gunning the car out of the subdivision. In less than fifteen minutes was back in his motel room, gulping vodka.

Joe glared out the window at the traffic roaring by on the Airport Expressway less than a hundred yards away. He was deflated. So much time and effort had gone into his master plan, and he was within a few feet of fulfilling it to perfection. The more he brooded, the more he drank. After two hours and a fifth of vodka the relentless craving for cocaine came calling. Cocaine was his best friend and had been summoning him all day, but he had resisted answering the call because he was on a mission. With his plans in shambles, he pulled a small baggie partially filled with a fine white powder out of his Dopp kit and poured it into a fresh fifth of 100-proof Stolichnaya vodka he had been saving for the post-slaughter celebration. In less than an hour he was comatose on the floor next to the bed.

Holloway lay on the floor in his motel room for almost eight hours, too wrecked to move. When he finally woke up, he barely made it to the bathroom before he threw up. His head was pounding, his hands were shaking, and there was a little blood in the sink after the prolonged coughing spell. He gulped down another glass of cocaine-flavored vodka and passed out again for three more hours.

When Joe jerked awake, his thinking was a little crisper. Sitting in the only chair in the room, he began restructuring his mission. After considering his options, he decided he could resurrect the plan by simply returning to Colleyville. Weasel's snitching to the cops had not paid off. He had outsmarted them again and slipped through the dragnet they had cast for him. The police surely had been devastated by his cleverness, and failing to catch him, the lazy foolish cops would have given up and left. All he had to do was return to the house and shoot everyone. Why had he gotten himself so worked up? The answer was simple. He fell into the car and headed back toward Colleyville. At Cheek Sparger Road he turned east to Mockingbird Lane. Once again he slowly rolled down the hill toward Saddlebrook Drive, and once again the scene at the Graham house caused him to stop short of the target.

This time there were three police cars parked in front of the house and several armed uniformed officers standing on the porch near the front door. Holy shit! What is going on here? Are these guys all living in the house? How many cops could there be in there? In his deluded state, Holloway misunderstood what he saw. In reality, the group on the front porch consisted of a Tarrant County sheriff visiting a moonlighting fellow deputy on assignment with Texas Corporate Protection. Two TCP cars were parked in the circular drive, and the deputy's marked Ford Explorer was sitting street-side along the curb. The cops standing vigil on the porch were in fact two of Ragetty's uniformed agents shooting the bull with a visiting friend who just happened to drive a sheriff's patrol vehicle.

* * *

Back at the motel Holloway was in a foul rage. He hurled a lamp at the television, sending chunks of glass flying in every direction. He kicked the plastic wastebasket across the room into a large oval mirror hanging over the credenza along the wall. How could he possibly be expected to carry out his mission if every law enforcement officer in Tarrant County was guarding Sonny Graham? The Colleyville situation was hopeless, but it was no fault of his. He had tried to stick to the blueprint.

He suddenly paused from wreaking havoc on the motel room. Wait just a minute. He had forgotten that he had developed a backup plan for just such an occasion. Just like that, Joe was back on track and knew exactly what he needed to do. He loaded all the weapons, ammo, booze and drugs in his room into the car and left the parking lot without notifying the front desk that he was checking out. The La Quinta Inn could settle up with Claude and Dalotta whenever it wanted.

* * *

The holidays were rapidly approaching. Sonny and Joan weren't looking forward to the discussion but knew they had to have a heart-to-heart talk with the kids about how different this year's celebrations would be from years past. Rather than having family in for a feast, they would be celebrating Thanksgiving by themselves. Santa would still be able to find their house on Christmas Eve, but that whole extravaganza would be scaled way back. There would be no Christmas lights on the house or caroling in the neighborhood this year because it would be too dangerous to walk around outside. Joan choked back tears as Sonny tried desperately to put a smiley face on a disappointing situation for the kids. Logan bought the whole story, but Wren was mature enough to realize that Dad was trying to put a silk bow on a dirty pig.

It was a small positive that Logan didn't recognize the gravity of the situation. To his thinking, the Holloway affair was some sort of holiday. He didn't have to go to preschool, he had a new pet dog, and he got to play soccer in the house. He was a happy camper. Wren, however, acknowledged in her own way that she understood that there was a big problem. Having just been told that many of their family's traditional holiday events would be cancelled, Wren innocently asked whether they could invite the guards to Thanksgiving dinner. She was pleased when Sonny assured her they would be there. Later that day, Wren colored a drawing for her parents showing the family around the Christmas decorations. Big Mike and Danny were there, too, smiling stick figures standing sentry by the tree.

When Sonny first explained why they had had to move to Granbury, he wanted to be truthful but not scare his little girl. He told Wren that a bad man might try to hurt the family so they were going away for a short time until it was safe to come back home. Wren had asked why Holloway was a bad man, and Sonny simply said that he took drugs and drank so much alcohol that he didn't know what he was doing. Wren, fresh off school health lessons on the perils of cigarettes, understood. "I bet he smokes, too," she said.

* * *

John Ragetty and Danny Peters stopped by the house the day before Thanksgiving and brought the Grahams a large basket full of fruit, nuts, candies, and gourmet coffees and teas. They also brought a couple of plush stuffed animals for the kids. There had always been a pleasant exchange between the group that at first had been friendly out of necessity but now was due to genuine enjoyment of one another. Ragetty and Peters both had children about the same age as Wren and Logan, and though they admired how the Graham family was standing tough under pressure, it hurt both men to know the terrible toll the situation was taking on the family.

After a few minutes of pleasantries, Ragetty got around to the real reason for the visit. He had done everything he could and played every card he had, but Korman had finally followed through on his threat to end the security detail. Omniplex was cancelling Texas Corporate Protection's contract and the Grahams' security detail at the end of the year.

Ragetty knew how hard this development would hit Sonny and Joan, and he hated to bring such bad news. But he decided to confidentially tip them off in person the day after Michael Opperman called to tell him the decision. Opperman had reached out to tip off Ragetty about the notice that Aaron Silverstein would be delivering in writing to Sonny right after Christmas. The carefully crafted document waiving liability would be packed full of approved legalese with the full intention of leaving Omniplex with as much future wiggle room as possible.

With genuine sadness in his voice, Opperman had told Ragetty that he had tried his best to fight the decision but had gone down swinging. He had appeared before the board to make a case against Korman, but he simply lacked the horsepower to outrun him. The Japanese had no real reference point to evaluate the security risk, and the board could not fathom the potential catastrophe about which

Opperman spoke. None of the Japanese could grasp that a massacre could take place at Omniplex; in Japan such an action would be unthinkable. Korman had framed his argument purely as a matter of money. The board respected Opperman's abilities and appreciated his loyalty to a valuable employee, but despite his impassioned pleas, the decision was about the money.

Sonny and Joan took the news stoically. They knew this day might come but had hoped they would have more time before being left on their own. Sonny knew the buyout proposal had been stillborn but secretly held out hopes for the transfer to England. He asked Ragetty what percentage he would put on a transfer taking place. Ragetty didn't hesitate to answer: "Zero."

To try to soften the blow, Ragetty said he would do what he could to drag the separation out as much as possible. He believed he could convince Omniplex that it would take some time to close down the operation, which would buy them a couple weeks. He could also leave the empty mobile command post in place in the driveway for a month or so. The trailer was rented through February and wasn't needed for another assignment. With it still in place, Holloway might assume that security was still active even though Ragetty would have to pull his guards off the case on New Year's Eve. Last, and most touching,

Ragetty told Sonny and Joan that Danny, Big Mike and Hoppy had volunteered to drive by the house on their way to and from other assignments. For a while at least, Ragetty's men would still be randomly showing up to see the Grahams.

TWENTY-FIVE

It was a cool but sunny Tuesday in early December 1991 with the hint of a breeze in St. John the Baptist Parish, Louisiana, as a dark-blue Oldsmobile Calais wheeled into the Riverlands Professional Plaza parking lot near the end of the work day. A well-groomed man in a gray tweed sport coat was driving. His passenger in the front seat was a petite, dark-haired woman wearing a pink silk dress. The car slowly moved through the rows of vacant parking spaces and pulled up at the curb in front of The Times-Picayune newspaper's River Parishes Bureau office. The driver stopped the car directly adjacent to the front door of the newspaper.

Warren Roberts, a veteran reporter at the news bureau, was writing at his cluttered desk and looked up to see the Oldsmobile stop near the front door, pointed into the oncoming traffic lane. The scene caught his attention because no one immediately got out of the car to come into the office. He gazed at the car and the people inside, who appeared to be talking. After a few moments, he returned his attention to his work. He had only briefly resumed his writing when he heard a scream from the parking lot loud enough to penetrate the bureau's plate-glass windows.

As Roberts looked up for a second time he saw a bright flash from the front seat of the car and heard the unmistakable report of a gunshot. He bolted toward the office entrance, several colleagues following him, but just as the group opened the double doors, additional explosive pops were heard from the car. Everyone scurried back inside the office and took cover behind desks and filing cabinets, unsure what was happening. In the confusion, some feared there was a shooter on the roof of the building. For a few minutes, employees of the Times-Picayune crouched behind their desks waiting for more rounds to be fired, but nothing happened for several minutes. Then, suddenly, there was another blast from the car, followed by silence.

Within a few minutes, people from other offices in the plaza started moving toward the parked car, and soon a small crowd of curious onlookers had gathered near the vehicle. Shifting into reporter mode, Warren Roberts was one of the first to the scene. Looking through the open driver's side window, Roberts observed a bizarre sight, as the two adults in the front seat were slumped forward, the woman's head on the man's right shoulder and the driver's head on the steering wheel. Both were obviously dead. Still in the driver's left hand was a silver-gray snub-nosed .38-caliber revolver. A custom-made left-handed shotgun, protruding from an unzipped, blood-covered, brown-leather gun case, lay across the driver's lap. His right hand rested on the barrel of the shotgun, which was pointed at the passenger side of the car. Heavy blood splatter speckled the front window of the car, and a whiff of blue-gray gun smoke floated from the open driver's side window.

As the crowd grew, people pressed toward the car to get a better look at the eerie spectacle. Phone calls flooded into the local emergency number, and less than three minutes after the last shot was fired the first St. John the Baptist Parish sheriff's car roared into the parking lot with sirens blaring and lights flashing. Soon the professional plaza was crawling with law enforcement like flies on road kill. Officers cordoned off the crime scene and moved the now large, silent crowd away from the death vehicle. A sheriff's department photographer began taking pictures of the car from every conceivable angle as detectives fanned out to look for evidence and witnesses. It didn't take long for them to find someone who had seen the entire incident.

Mel Ridenhour, a lawyer and part owner of the professional plaza, was getting paperwork from his briefcase from the trunk of his car parked just four spaces from the traffic lane where the shooting occurred. He was looking directly at the vehicle as the grizzly drama unfolded. Ridenhour first told the detectives, then later repeated the same story to Warren Roberts, that he had observed the dark-blue car as it pulled to the curb.

After the Oldsmobile came to a stop, there was a moment of silence. Then, suddenly, loud shouting came from the car. Shortly after, the front passenger door popped opened, and a well-dressed middle-aged woman scrambled out of the car and started to run around the front. Before she got more than a couple feet away, the driver jumped out, ran her down and forcibly escorted her to the car and back into the front passenger seat. The driver shut the passenger side door, then quickly rounded the front of the car to get back behind the wheel, slamming the car door after him. Again, there were a few moments of quiet, when suddenly a chilling, piercing scream interrupted the silence, quickly followed by a single booming gun shot. Ridenhour ducked beside his car, looking over the trunk as two more quick shots were fired. Silence again, and people started emerging from surrounding offices. Then, as Ridenhour looked on and a small band of bystanders began moving toward the car, a final shot rang out.

* * *

Tuesday evening, December 3, 1991, at approximately 9:40 p.m., Sonny and Joan Graham were just settling into the upholstered Lay-Z-Boy chairs in the family room after getting Wren and Logan into bed for the night when the phone rang. Joan shot Sonny a perplexed look. They rarely received late-evening phone calls. Most of their friends had children who also went to bed before 10 p.m. and wouldn't call that late. Sonny got up and grabbed the phone on the wall in the kitchen.

After answering the phone, Sonny stood in the kitchen for several minutes without saying anything, simply listening to the caller. His brow was pinched, and he seemed to be trying to fully absorb every word he was hearing. Joan, sensing something might be wrong, got up and walked to his side. She couldn't hear anything the caller was saying, but it was clear to her that something important was being discussed. Sonny shot her a quick glace, then turned his back to her as if to signal that he didn't want to be distracted.

After what seemed like an eternity to Joan, Sonny thanked the caller and looked at the receiver before hanging up. He slowly turned toward his wife.

"What? What is it?" she pleaded.

Sonny smiled broadly, gave her a bear hug and said, "Baby, we're going to have a great Christmas."

TWENTY-SIX

John Ragetty pulled his new dark-green Jaguar into the Grahams' circular drive a half-hour after the phone call. Sonny and Joan met him at the front door, and the three quickly exchanged hugs in the entryway before they went into the house. Ragetty wasted no time cutting to the chase. That evening at 8:15, Colleyville Police Chief Steel had called to advise Ragetty of a call he had just received from the St. John the Baptist Parish sheriff's department in LaPlace, Louisiana.

Chief Steel relayed information provided by Deputy Roman Ober regarding a shooting that had occurred earlier in the day at the Riverlands Professional Plaza in LaPlace. According to Ober, a middle-age white male driving a dark-blue Oldsmobile Calais had parked in the plaza and shot and killed a white female passenger before committing suicide. The woman had been identified as Melissa Gier Holloway of Metairie, Louisiana. The driver carried no identification and had only several .38-caliber shells in his pockets. He had yet to be identified, but the police were moving forward on the assumption that the killer was Melissa Holloway's ex-husband, Joseph Vincent Holloway. Ober had called Colleyville to obtain Holloway's fingerprints to use to identify the driver. After Ober's call to Colleyville, Detective Mortan had alerted Ragetty, and Ragetty called Sonny right away.

The Grahams were relieved at the confirmation of the cursory information Ragetty had related during the phone call less than an hour earlier, but he told them that, though there was every indication the shooter had been Holloway, nothing would be official until an autopsy was performed. The medical examiner had told Ragetty that it would take place within the coming week.

A half-hour later, Sonny walked Ragetty to the door, and as they stepped onto the front porch, Sonny suddenly became serious. In a hushed voice so that Joan wouldn't overhear, he said, "John, I can't wait a week or more to know for sure if it really is Holloway. I need to find out tomorrow because if it isn't him, it'll destroy Joan. She thinks this nightmare is over. Is there any way you can get the autopsy faster?"

Ragetty frowned and thought for a minute. "A guy who used to work for me lives in Metairie," he said. "I'll call him in the morning and have him drive over to the funeral home where they took the body and get one of the morticians to take a set of fingerprints off the corpse. He can fax them to me, and I'll have a guy I know over at the Texas Ranger's office run them for me. Joe has a military record, and his fingerprints will be on file." Sonny was surprised. "You can do that?" he asked incredulously. "Is that legal? How can you do that?" As John opened his car door he laughed and said, "Don't worry. I'll give 'em a couple tickets to a Cowboys game."

The next afternoon Ragetty called Sonny and said simply, "It's him." Sonny breathed a sigh of relief, then found himself struggling with a mix of emotions. He was glad Holloway was dead, he told Ragetty. He would never grieve for him. After what Holloway had put the family through, Sonny was thankful that he wouldn't be tormenting them any longer.

But Sonny was panged with sadness that Melissa, an innocent victim, had died. Ragetty understood Sonny's feelings, but then he told Sonny something that quickly brought his focus back to his family. They weren't out of the woods yet. Sonny was stunned. How could this not be over now that Holloway was dead? Sonny closed his eyes and silently mouthed, "Now what?"

"After I got Holloway's prints," Ragetty said, "I called back Deputy Ober in LaPlace and got some additional details on the incident. The murder-suicide occurred just as it was reported. But during the initial investigation police learned that Holloway had been staying at a motel in Metairie. They went to the Peacock Motor Inn on Veteran's Highway, which is a $30-a-night fleabag hangout for addicts and dope dealers. It's a run-down, long-stay motel with no maid service. When the cops searched Holloway's room, what they found gave even the most seasoned officers some pause."

Ragetty told Sonny the motel room was trashed with fast food containers, empty liquor bottles and porn magazines. Police also found military survival manuals, food supplies, ammunition and a cache of weapons. Deputy Ober had told Ragetty that there were more than a dozen handguns, ten knives and six high-powered rifles in the small, shabby room. Ragetty then told Sonny that it was what the police didn't find that was the problem.

The St. John the Baptist sheriff's department had discovered several books on bomb-making, one specifically on how to make small letter bombs that could be sent through the mail. There was also an indication that Holloway had been making bombs in the room, as several partially completed explosive devices had been discovered. There was a stack of addressed envelopes in the room, all containing threatening and vile messages addressed to Sonny, and there was information that led the detectives to believe that Holloway had hired someone to help him kill Sonny. Police were concerned that they hadn't found completed bombs.

The deputies were equally worried that they had found several empty business envelopes addressed to Wren and Logan, which appeared to be part of a test run of Holloway's letter-bomb enterprise. Sonny slumped forward in his chair and let his hand holding the phone fall forward into his lap. When would it end? Now Holloway was reaching out from the grave in an attempt to harm his children.

Ragetty tried to reassure him that things weren't as bleak as they seemed. He had already worked out an arrangement with the Colleyville Post Office for a mail hold for the next sixty days. The post office would hold their mail for a week at a time and run it through an X-ray machine before delivering it to the house. Any suspicious letters or packages would trigger a call to the Tarrant County sheriff's bomb squad. Ragetty calmingly said there was almost no chance that a letter bomb could get delivered to the house, but then he quickly added that just to be safe,

Sonny should coach Joan and the kids not to open any letters or packages unless they arrived hand-delivered directly from the post office in the weekly mail drop. Sonny listened, but he didn't tell Ragetty that Holloway's after-death strategy had already been initiated. He had received a threatening phone call on his office phone just hours after Joe had killed himself.

During the next three weeks, Sonny received seven intimidating phone messages on the answering machine connected to his business line at home. Each time, the caller would leave the same message promising that Sonny would soon be a dead man. He knew there was no point trying to have the calls traced as they never lasted more than a couple seconds, and it was obvious the caller was disguising his voice. He was disturbed by the calls, but in his gut he knew they couldn't hurt him. They were designed to torment him, and Sonny never really believed he was in danger from the mysterious caller. Ragetty had told him about the friends Holloway had made in jail and that they were losers just like Joe. Sonny couldn't believe one of them would kill on behalf of a dead man because he had been paid a pack of cigarettes.

* * *

The Grahams' life gradually started to return to normal. The mail was dropped off once a week by special delivery from the post office, but there had never been any suspicious items, and nothing had ever been found by X-raying all the letters and packages. The fast-approaching holidays took on new meaning for the family, and they baked cookies, decorated the house and played Christmas music all day.

The week after the murder-suicide, Sonny started going into the office every day. It wasn't exactly business as usual, but he was far more productive and involved in daily operations than he had been in many months. A week later, Wren was back in elementary school and Logan was on the swings at his pre-school. Three weeks later, for the first time in more than a year, Joan had her first ladies' tea at the house. By the end of the year, the family was enjoying the unusually warm December having cookouts on the pool deck, and the kids were playing freely with the dog in the back yard.

Three months passed, and there was barely a sign of the turmoil the Grahams had endured. Ragetty's mobile command center had been removed weeks earlier. All the security guards were gone. Danny, Big Mike and Hoppy weren't dropping by unannounced. The Colleyville Post Office had stopped X-raying their mail, and random police cars were no longer parked in the Grahams' driveway. Best of all, the harassing phone calls had stopped. Sonny hadn't heard from the shadowy telephone stalker in seven weeks.

One night while sitting around the table during dinner, Wren asked about the security guards. She missed Big Mike and Danny and wondered whether she would ever see them again.

But then she thought for a moment. And with the wisdom of someone far beyond her years, she said, "I guess we really don't want them to *have* to come back."

EPILOGUE

As time passed, the once-vivid memories of the havoc and destruction caused by Joe Holloway's year of terror faded from the minds of many of those involved. For Sonny and Joan Graham, however, the event was a surreal nightmare that remained a fresh memory and would never totally be banished from their psyches. In the years after Holloway's suicide, some of those involved faired far better than others.

Lester Newcastle:
Weasel did Holloway's bidding for a short time after Holloway left Texas out of fear that Joe might return and make good on his promise to kill him. Weasel

tormented Sonny by phone until he learned that Holloway was dead, then immediately ended the harassment. He never really had a strong commitment to the project and wasn't about to do anything other than make a few phone calls. Short on cash and out of work, he took a job as a fry cook at a greasy spoon in the Fort Worth suburb of Haltom City. Weasel didn't last long on the job before being sacked for stealing food from the supply room. He moved on to work on the loading dock at a Staples Office Supply distribution warehouse for northern Tarrant County, but he soon was observed on security videos loading dozens of new ink-jet printers into his beat-up van. He is back in Greenbay in the Tarrant County Jail.

Nelson Smith:

Snuffy's knife job on Ruby in the Tarrant County Jail earned him an additional twelve months in the slammer. During a mandated anger-management counseling session, he met a young Hispanic woman who had volunteered through her church to serve refreshments to the inmates. Snuffy and María Alejandra Lopez hit it off immediately, and she started visiting him at Greenbay. After his release from prison, Snuffy and Maria Alejandra moved in together. Although, he'd never been inclined to embrace religion of any kind, Snuffy was soon attending Our Lady of Holy Mercy Church in Lake

Worth with Lopez. One year to the day after his release from prison, the Rev. Luis Alvarez married Nelson Grant Smith and Maria Alejandra Lopez at Our Lady of Holy Mercy. The wedding ceremony was immediately followed by Snuffy's baptism. With the help of the church, Snuffy got a job on the midnight maintenance crew at Bell Helicopter's manufacturing plant in Fort Worth, where he worked his way up to shift supervisor. He and Maria Alejandra have two well-adjusted children and a small home in North Richland Hills, Texas.

Lucas Westwright:

Joe's dimwitted friend from the Brothers of the Red X served twelve years in prison on a variety of charges and was paroled eight years after Holloway's death. Lacking any marketable skills, he immediately returned to a life of crime to fuel a raging drug habit and quickly spiraled downhill. He was killed in a shootout with police during a botched pharmacy robbery.

Jay Draper:

Jay stayed with Omniplex and continued working for Sonny for three years until he was recruited to run a small medical products supply company in Jackson,

Mississippi. He successfully ran the company for a couple years but left after a dispute over short-term business strategy with the board of directors. Sonny connected Jay with a health services company in Nashville, Tennessee, that hired him as CEO. Jay runs that multi-million-dollar corporation and lives on a gentleman's farm just outside the Music City with his wife and three children.

Johnny Jay Lovett:

Attorney Lovett continued his flamboyant and lucrative legal practice. In the years after working for Omniplex on the Holloway affair, he represented some of the highest-profile criminal cases in the Dallas-Fort Worth Metroplex. Johnny Jay twice unsuccessfully ran for a seat on the Fort Worth City Council and was roundly defeated in an attempt to win election as mayor. Never one to acknowledge defeat, he recently hinted that he was considering a run for a state Senate seat.

Tarrant County District Attorney Chet McKinney:

McKinney retired after having served as the county's district attorney for thirty years. Initially praised for his years of dedicated service, he was later found to have unethically manipulated cases, illegally withheld critical evidence and improperly used government resources. For a short while there was an outcry from some politicians to indict McKinney; however, the uproar soon faded, as did his carefully constructed reputation. Shunned by many of his fellow barristers, he retired to a large waterfront home on Eagle Mountain Lake near Fort Worth, where he currently lives with his wife.

Tarrant County Sheriff Tag Johnson: After the Holloway incident, Johnson won re-election and served another term as sheriff. During his final six months in office he was diagnosed with pancreatic cancer and died a year later.

Colleyville Police Chief Drake Steel: Steel retired from police work shortly after the conclusion of the Holloway matter. He moved back to his hometown of Lubbock, Texas, where he bought a 25-acre ranch. He breeds show dogs and runs the largest animal kennel in western Texas.

Danny Peters:
Peters remained with Texas Corporate Protection after Ragetty sold the company, but he was seriously injured while on duty a year and a half later. Peters was working a security contract for a wealthy Dallas businessman when he fell from a retaining wall while checking perimeter security at the estate. After a long

recovery he returned to administrative work at TCP. When John Ragetty formed his new company, Peters signed on as vice president of field operations. He still works with Ragetty.

Michael "Big Mike" Knight:
Mike stayed with Texas Corporate Protection for three years after the Omniplex assignment but left the company for full-time police work with the Arlington Police Department. Cited several times for bravery as a patrol officer, he was eventually promoted to shift supervisor. A few months later while sitting in his marked police vehicle with red lights fully illuminated at a routine traffic stop, he was killed when a 92-year-old man stepped on the gas rather than the brake and lost control of his car. The elderly driver slammed into the back of Big Mike's patrol car at more than 75 mph, and he was killed instantly. Knight was given a hero's funeral with officers from all over the Dallas area attending the service.

John Ragetty:
Ragetty continued to run Texas Corporate Protection for five more years, attracting high-value clients and handling serious security matters. Eventually, he tired of the high-pressure grind and sold his interest in the company to a competitor from St. Louis. With his wife, Ragetty then opened a bed and breakfast in a

historic old home in Granbury, but the business failed during an economic downturn. Returning to the origin of his major success, Ragetty launched a new corporate security firm, partnering with an associate who had served as assistant director of the FBI. The company has flourished, and Ragetty occasionally appears on TV news programs as an expert security analyst.

Sidney Korman:

Korman continued to bully his subordinates at Omniplex Worldwide for several years. As the medical products industry changed during the mid-'90s with a national trend toward keeping costs down in managed care, Omniplex's high-end product line experienced a significant decline in market share. Korman began to take heat for his leadership style and lack of results. When his handpicked subordinate, Mark Tyler, was caught cheating the federal government on medical products contracts, the Omniplex Worldwide board of directors blamed Korman for his poor judgment. The man whose credo was that the only thing that mattered was the bottom line was done in by a $30 million federal fine. Korman's star rapidly fell after that, and he soon lost a no-confidence vote by the board. The day before Korman was to meet with an Omniplex legal team, headed by corporate attorney Aaron Silverstein, to begin negotiating his departure from the company, he was found sitting at his desk in his opulent office with his head face-down in a newspaper. He had died instantly from a massive heart attack. No one from Omniplex attended his funeral, not even his long-time personal assistant Dorothy Stillman.

Mark Tyler:

Ever the shrewd corporate gamesman, Tyler bided his time as senior vice president at Omniplex while currying favor with Korman. Upon Michael Opperman's departure, Tyler ascended to the position he had long coveted and was named president of the Medical Products Group by Korman. However, his tenure as president was very short. Less than a year into the job, Tyler was unceremoniously fired after Omniplex was charged with circumventing the provisions of a U.S. government contract. The company was forced to pay a $30 million fine to avoid a lengthy and costly court battle they probably would have lost. Known throughout the industry for being devious, self-serving, arrogant and difficult, Tyler had problems finding another job, but eventually landed an executive position with a medical products start-up. But that company went bankrupt in less than two years, and he was again out of work. He is divorced, unemployed and living on his Omniplex pension in upstate New York with Kelly Upton, his former administrative assistant.

Michael Opperman:

The President of Omniplex Worldwide's Medical Products Group continued to lead the endoscope division for several years but paid a significant price for having challenged the corporate president's wisdom over the handling of the Holloway affair. Opperman's career was deadended, and he met increased resistance and interference from Korman as the years went by. Tiring of the frustration, he unexpectedly resigned his position and retired to an expensive home on Long Island. He loves fly-fishing and spends much of his time traveling the globe on fishing trips.

Ronald Holloway:

Ronald disavowed any responsibility for the actions of his brother and never talked publicly about his death. He refused to pay for Joe's body to be taken to Florida for burial. He continued in his successful real estate law practice for three years after Joe's suicide but started drinking heavily. After a gala charity fund-raising event, Ronald was killed in a traffic accident in Tampa. With a blood-alcohol level almost three times the legal limit, he drove through a red light and was broadsided by a semi-truck.

Vonda Stone Holloway:

Her mind ravaged by dementia and her life savings siphoned off by Joe, Vonda was left to rely on the kindness of her elder son, Ronald. Ronald paid for her care in a privately operated memory-care facility but never visited her and made no provisions for her beyond a month-to-month payment for her care. When Ronald was killed in the auto accident, she was left without a benefactor and ended up on public assistance, living out the last two years of her life nearly comatose in a state-run nursing home.

Kimberly Holloway Vanderguard:

Joe and Melissa's daughter was a sophomore at the University of Texas in Austin when her parents died. Although they did not leave her financially comfortable, years earlier Joe had prepaid a small life insurance policy that named his wife, Melissa, as beneficiary. Upon her murder, the $35,000 death benefit was paid to Kimberly. The funds were enough, along with the money she earned working as a waitress at an Austin tavern, for her to finish college with a degree in finance. She remained in Austin after graduation and worked as an accountant for a small computer company, where she met Carey Vanderguard, a computer programmer from

Weatherford, Texas. They married, have three children and still live in Austin.

Melissa Gier Holloway:

After her murder, Melissa Holloway's parents had her remains returned to their hometown of Evansville, Indiana, for burial. Kimberly returned to Indiana for the funeral, which was attended by nearly 100 people, most of whom had known Melissa since childhood.

Joseph Vincent Holloway:

After his suicide, Holloway's body was taken to a funeral home in LaPlace, Louisiana, for autopsy and to establish his identity. No one from his family claimed the remains, which eventually were cremated at state expense and interred in a pauper's cemetery in St. Charles Parish, Louisiana.

Logan Graham:

Sonny and Joan's son followed in his sister's academic footsteps and graduated at the top of his high school class, finishing eleventh in a class of 718. He was a standout athlete in multiple sports as a youth but concentrated on soccer in high school, where he was captain of the varsity soccer team for three years and twice was honored as an All District player. Logan was also captain of his select level competitive soccer team and played on a team that finished runner-up in the North American Indoor Soccer Championships. He was selected to play on the United States Soccer Association's North Texas team in the U.S. Olympic Development Program. When he graduated from high school, Logan received an appointment to the U.S. Military Academy in West Point, New York. He finished in the top ten percent of his class, and after graduation entered active duty with the Army, serving three tours of duty in the Middle East. Maj. Graham recently fulfilled a long-standing desire by returning to West Point as a professor of American history. Logan married Beth Cranston, also from Colleyville. They have one daughter.

Wren Graham:

Sonny and Joan's daughter excelled in school in both academics and athletics. She was captain of the high school swim team but also played softball and soccer. She ranked as a top ten student in a graduating class of 695 and was named Miss Congeniality her senior year. Wren was recognized as one of President George H.W. Bush's "Thousand Points of Light" for outstanding volunteerism and charity work. She earned a four-year scholarship to Vanderbilt University in Nashville, then moved to Washington, D.C., where she worked in the hospitality industry before taking a job coordinating marketing events for a major worldwide software company.

Joan Graham:

Joan raised her two children as a stay-at-home mom for several years. She nurtured them well and gave them a great start in life. After the kids had successfully established themselves in school, she accepted an offer to manage a large medical practice, assuming control of every facet of the business operation. She was efficient, organized and an excellent taskmaster, but more important, loved by the patients. She retired after serving the practice for 15 years and moved to Rancho Santa Margarita, California, with Sonny.

Sonny Graham:

After the Holloway affair, Sonny continued his employment with Omniplex Worldwide before retiring after twenty years of service. After he successfully formed and led the Family Practice Products Group, he went on to develop and manage an innovative and award-winning nurse consulting and physician training division for the company. After retiring from Omniplex, Sonny became a medical products industry consultant working with foreign companies new to the U.S. market. After two years he was appointed chief executive officer of QueBuy International Inc., a publicly traded company headquartered in Toronto, Canada. QueBuy was a boutique software engineering firm that specialized in developing smart-card payment systems. When Sonny assumed leadership of the company, QueBuy was in pre-bankruptcy, having been closed by the Canadian government for being severely behind in tax payments. He raised $8 million in venture capital for the firm and stabilized the business. Sonny served six years as CEO of QueBuy before retiring. However, less than a year later, Sonny made one more stop before completely retreating from the business world, when he was appointed a Tarrant County property tax arbitrator. Based on the scope of his high-level business career, he was certified by the state to sit as an Appraisal Review Board judge for tax disputes. During his time with the review board, Sonny handled some of the largest tax challenges filed in the county, once ruling on a $750 million oil and gas grievance. He resigned from the board after three years and moved to Orange County, California, with Joan, where they live in a golf course retirement community in Rancho Santa Margarita.